SILENT NEIGHBOR

BLAKE PIERCE

Blake Pierce is author of the bestselling RILEY PAGE mystery series, which includes fifteen books (and counting). Blake Pierce is also the author of the MACKENZIE WHITE mystery series, comprising thirteen books (and counting); of the AVERY BLACK mystery series, comprising six books; of the KERI LOCKE mystery series, comprising five books; of the MAKING OF RILEY PAIGE mystery series, comprising four books (and counting); of the KATE WISE mystery series, comprising five books (and counting); of the CHLOE FINE psychological suspense mystery, comprising five books (and counting); and of the JESSE HUNT psychological suspense thriller series, comprising five books (and counting).

ONCE GONE (a Riley Paige Mystery—Book #1), BEFORE HE KILLS (A Mackenzie White Mystery—Book 1), CAUSE TO KILL (An Avery Black Mystery—Book 1), A TRACE OF DEATH (A Keri Locke Mystery—Book 1), and WATCHING (The Making of Riley Paige—Book 1) are each available as a free download on Amazon!

An avid reader and lifelong fan of the mystery and thriller genres, Blake loves to hear from you, so please feel free to visit www.blakepierceauthor.com to learn more and stay in touch.

BOOKS BY BLAKE PIERCE

A JESSIE HUNT PSYCHOLOGICAL SUSPENSE SERIES
THE PERFECT WIFE (Book #1)
THE PERFECT BLOCK (Book #2)
THE PERFECT HOUSE (Book #3)
THE PERFECT SMILE (Book #4)
THE PERFECT LIE (Book 35)

CHLOE FINE PSYCHOLOGICAL SUSPENSE SERIES
NEXT DOOR (Book #1)
A NEIGHBOR'S LIE (Book #2)
CUL DE SAC (Book #3)
SILENT NEIGHBOR (Book #4)
HOMECOMING (Book #5)

KATE WISE MYSTERY SERIES
IF SHE KNEW (Book #1)
IF SHE SAW (Book #2)
IF SHE RAN (Book #3)
IF SHE HID (Book #4)
IF SHE FLED (Book #5)

THE MAKING OF RILEY PAIGE SERIES
WATCHING (Book #1)
WAITING (Book #2)
LURING (Book #3)
TAKING (Book #4)

SILENT NEIGHBOR

(A Chloe Fine Psychological Suspense Mystery—Book 4)

BLAKE PIERCE

TABLE OF CONTENTS

PROLOGUE

Rosa unlocked the door to the two-story home, thinking how strange it was that people hired other people to clean their homes, giving them full access to every room and potential secret to their lives. Rosa had been cleaning homes in the Falls Church, Virginia area for six years now and she had stumbled upon quite a few unexpected things. It alarmed her just how little people did to cover up their indiscretions and secrets.

She didn't think she was going to accidentally find scandalous items or dark secrets with this couple, though. This was her newest client—the seventh on her list, helping her to hit her goal of making four grand a month by just cleaning houses. Not too bad for a woman who had once barely paid her three-hundred-fifty-dollar rent by bussing tables.

No, this couple, the Fairchilds, seemed clean-cut and free of drama. A nice married couple, though possibly a bit too involved in their work. The husband was some sort of finance broker who traveled at least once a month to attend meetings in New York and Boston. The wife, a mousy-looking woman of fifty or so, didn't seem to actually do much of anything. She was some sort of social media influencer—whatever that meant. But they were nice enough, they were wealthy, and they were incredibly kind and friendly to Rosa ... something that a lot of her other clients were not.

She stepped inside the large foyer and glanced around at the spacious living room, the open floor plan and the attached kitchen, separated only by a floating bar. The house was, in her opinion, far too big for a couple with no kids—a couple where the husband was gone about a week or so out of every month.

Taking a look around, Rosa figured this would be one of those weeks where she was going to feel as if she wasn't truly earning her money. The Fairchilds were quite neat, leaving the house mostly clean. Rosa would go through the motions, scrubbing and vacuuming and cleaning windows, but it really wasn't much of a chore in the Fairchild house.

She went to the laundry room and the adjoining mudroom, where she filled the utility sink with water, dumping a bit of lavender-scented Pine Sol into it. She figured she'd get the kitchen floors, as it seemed to be the most-used room in the house. While she was waiting for the floors to dry, she'd vacuum the upstairs rooms, all of which were carpeted. She hated to feel as if she was getting one over on such a nice couple, but she figured if she could make it appear that she had truly gotten all of the most important areas, the Fairchilds would consider it a job well done. Besides, it wasn't her fault that they were leaving practically nothing to clean up.

As she waited for the sink to fill halfway, Rosa walked through the kitchen and to the stairway. The vacuum was in the upstairs linen closet because it was the only area in the house with carpet. She figured it might need a new filter and wanted to check now before she started mopping and forgot.

She found the vacuum in its usual place and checked the filter, finding that she had another few uses before it needed to be changed. While she had the vacuum out, she decided to roll it into the master bedroom. It was a huge room, complete with a fireplace, built-in bookshelves, and an adjoining bathroom that was larger than the living room in Rosa's apartment.

The bedroom door was open, so she stepped in without knocking. She often didn't know whether Mrs. Fairchild was home or not but had learned to knock whenever there was a closed door in the Fairchild home. She rolled the vacuum in but stopped after she took three steps into the room.

Mrs. Fairchild was on the bed, sleeping. This felt odd, as she was pretty sure Mrs. Fairchild woke up early and went for a run on most days. She nearly left the room, not wanting to wake her. But then she noticed two peculiar things at once.

First, Mrs. Fairchild was dressed in her running attire. Second, she was lying on top of the sheets, the bed freshly made.

Alarm bells started sounding in Rosa's head and instead of backing out of the room as she had originally intended, she felt herself stepping forward as if pushed by an invisible hand.

"Mrs. Fairchild?" she asked.

There was no answer. Mrs. Fairchild didn't even move in response.

Call the police, Rosa thought. *Call nine-one-one. This is not good… she's not just sleeping, and you know it.*

But she had to know. She took two more steps forward until Mrs. Fairchild's face came into view.

Her eyes were staring open, looking toward the window—unblinking. Her mouth was partially open. A pool of blood, still relatively fresh, stained the sheet just above her head. A grotesque slash mark was plainly visible along her neck.

Rose felt a little moan rise up in her throat. Her knees buckled a bit, but she managed to take a few steps backward. When she collided with the vacuum, she let out a shriek.

It took a considerable amount of effort to tear her eyes away from Mrs. Fairchild, but when she did, she quickly ran out of the room. She went to the kitchen bar where she had set down her phone, and called 911. As the dispatcher answered, Rosa was so horrified by what she had seen that she didn't stop to think about the utility sink in the mudroom, filling and filling by the second, close to overflowing.

CHAPTER ONE

Chloe had heard many cautionary tales about trying to keep a very broad fence between her personal life and her career. As a federal agent, things tended to get very sticky when the two worlds collided. But honestly, she had been living with the constant collision of those two worlds ever since she had graduated from the academy—thanks to her father's mental cat-and-mouse games.

She knew she spent far too much time speculating on her father and what he may or may not have done to her mother nearly eighteen years ago. Thanks to Danielle's discovery of her mother's journal, Chloe had been living the past few weeks in a haze of confusion. She now felt fairly confident that their father had killed their mother all those years ago. She had given him every benefit of the doubt up to this point—going so far as to try pinning her mother's murder on a scapegoat, Ruthanne Carwile.

But now she had it written in her mother's handwriting. Now she had more than enough evidence to truly feel her father was not only a killer—but that he had killed her mother.

It had hit her quite hard. While Chloe had done her best not to let it affect her work, it had consumed almost every free moment she had. She'd spent the first two weekends after the discovery dodging calls from everyone—from Danielle, from her partner, Agent Rhodes, and from her father.

All I have to do is make it public, she thought to herself time and time again. *Just go public, take it to the bureau, and take him down. Wrap up this sordid chapter of my life and put the bastard back behind bars.*

But that was risky. It could affect her own career. And, more than that, there was the little girl still defiant inside of her, a younger version of herself who insisted maybe there was something she was missing... that there was no way her father was really a murderer.

It was an internal fight that had her going into work with a hangover a few times. It had been just twenty days since she'd made the discovery in the journal. And even at work, though she remained professional and did not let her own personal demons interfere with her job, entries from the journal would pop up in her head.

He strangled me tonight... and he slapped me in the face. Before I knew what had happened, he pushed me against the wall and strangled me. He said if I ever disrespected him again, he'd kill me. He said he had something better lined up, some better woman and some better life...

The journal was on her coffee table. She left it there so she would always be reminded... and so she could not give herself the convenience of having it out of her sight. She kept it there as a reminder that she had been a fool—and that her father had been pulling the wool over her eyes for a very long time.

It was twenty days in, almost three whole weeks since she and Danielle had finally come together to the conclusion that their father had killed their mother, when Chloe considered just going to his apartment and killing him. It was a Saturday. She'd started drinking at eleven that morning, staring out of her apartment window as DC traffic trickled by beneath her.

She knew enough about how the system worked to make it look like a suicide. Or, if nothing else, she knew how to hide her tracks well. She could make sure he died without having anything traced back to her.

She had thought it out quite carefully. She had the stirring of a plan in her head, most of which was solid.

But that's lunacy, isn't it? she asked herself.

But then she thought of how thoroughly he'd had her fooled. She remembered how loyal she had been to him even when Danielle had tried warning her that their father was not the man she thought. And when all of that weighed on her brain, no … the idea of killing him did not seem so drastic after all.

She was daydreaming of pulling the trigger on her father and starting on her third beer of the day when a gentle knock sounded on her door. She cringed; her father had come by four times in the past twenty days but she had always stayed quiet on the other side. This knock was different, though—the heartbeat-like drumming pattern from the intro to "Closer" by Nine Inch Nails, one of Danielle's favorite songs. It was the telltale knock they had agreed upon so that Chloe would know it was her sister on the other side of the door.

With a weary smile, Chloe answered the door. Danielle was waiting on the other side, in mid-beat. She lowered her hands and offered her sister a smile. It felt weird; Danielle was usually the gloomy one that Chloe tried to cheer up. It had been that way for most of their lives, especially ever since Danielle had discovered what absolute jerks boys can be.

"Not sleeping well?" Danielle asked as she stepped inside and closed the door behind her.

"Not particularly," Chloe said. "Want a beer?"

"What time is it?"

"Noon? Or close to it …"

"Just one," Danielle said, eyeing her sister suspiciously.

Chloe was very much aware of how the roles had basically turned completely around for them. As she popped the top on a bottle and handed it to Danielle, she saw the concern in her sister's face. Which was fine … it showed that Danielle had grown. It showed that in the face of what they had discovered together, she could stand on her own two feet without her sister there to support her like she'd usually done.

"I know what you're thinking," Chloe said.

"No, you don't. I hate to say that I sort of like the Chloe that drinks before noon. I like this moody fuck-the-world Chloe. But I'd be a bad sister if I didn't tell you that I'm worried about you. You don't exactly have the personality to pull off the dark and brooding goth thing."

"Is that why you're here?" Chloe asked. "To tell me you're worried about me?"

"Partly. But there's something else. And I need you to bear with me for a second, okay?"

"Sure," Chloe said as they settled down on the couch with their beers. She spotted her mother's journal on the coffee table and her thoughts briefly went back to the sordid idea of killing her father. And it was then, with Danielle sitting across from her, that she knew she could never do it. She could fantasize and plan all she wanted, but she would never do it. She simply wasn't that sort of person.

"So, a while back, I remember watching this show … sort of like one of those *Unsolved Mysteries* deals," Danielle said.

"I hope this is going somewhere," Chloe interrupted.

"It is. Anyway … it was about this woman who saved her brother's life. See … they were identical twins. Born like five minutes apart or something like that. She's cooking dinner for her family one night and gets this sharp twinge in her mind … sort of like someone speaking to her. She had the overwhelming idea that her brother was in trouble. It was so strong that she stopped what she was doing and called him. When he didn't answer the phone, she called her brother's girlfriend. The girlfriend went over to the brother's house and found that someone had broken into his home and shot him. He was bleeding out when the girlfriend found him but she called nine-one-one and ended up saving his life. All based on this weird feeling his twin sister got."

"Okay…"

Danielle rolled her eyes. Chloe could tell that she was thinking very hard about the next words to come out of her mouth. "I got something like that about forty minutes ago," she said. "Not nearly as strong as that TV show made it sound, but it was there. It was strong enough. And it was … well, it was weird."

"No one broke in," Chloe said. "I haven't been shot."

"I can see that. But … I don't know. I had the weird twin-feeling. I felt like I had to be over here. Sorry if it sounds dumb. But … well, is there anything I might have prevented by showing up?"

4

Chloe shook her head no. But she thought: *Just stopping me from plotting out the murder of our father.* She gave a soft little laugh and sipped from her beer.

"You're not well," Danielle said. She nodded to the beer bottle. "How many of those will I find in the trash, empty?"

"Two. And I'm sorry…but who are you to be concerned about someone's drinking habits? I have a kettle to go with that pot."

"Oh, I don't care about the drinking. You self-medicate however you see fit. But I do know that self-medicating isn't you. It never has been. You're the logical one…the smart one. It's because you've delved into my old strategies for coping that I'm here. *That's* what has me worried."

"I'm fine, Danielle."

Danielle folded her arms and reclined back on the couch. If there had been any good-natured ribbing to the conversation, Chloe sensed it disappear in that simple gesture. Danielle's gaze had an icy feel to it.

"So you mean to tell me that the last year or so, with you proclaiming Dad's greatness to me…I just let that ride? You and I coming to a head several times for him, and you always going to bat for him. The way I see it, I deserve some honesty, Chloe. I'm not stupid. This bombshell with Dad has messed you up."

"Of course it has."

"So tell me what you're thinking. Tell me what we do now. If I'm being totally honest, I don't see why you haven't turned him in yet. Isn't the journal enough to convict him?"

"You don't think I've thought of that?" Chloe asked, starting to get slightly angry. "And no…the journal isn't enough. It could be enough to maybe reopen the case, but that's about it. There's no hard evidence…and the fact that there was already a trial and our father was put in prison and then let go makes it even harder. Throw Ruthanne Carwile's recent conviction in there, and it becomes one huge mess."

"So you're saying he's likely going to end up getting away with it?"

Chloe didn't give an answer. She downed the rest of her beer and walked into the kitchen. She opened the refrigerator door to retrieve another but then stopped. Slowly, she closed it again and leaned against the small kitchen counter.

"I'm aware that this is mostly my fault," Chloe said. It was hard to admit. The words tasted like acid in her mouth as they came out.

"I'm not here to blame you, Chloe."

"I know. But it's what you're thinking. And I don't blame you. Now that I've seen what's in that journal and sort of…I don't know…sort of *have a feel for him*…I'm thinking it, too. If I had listened to you before all of this started it would be different. Before Ruthanne, before landing my job at the bureau…"

"Don't do that. Just…let's look forward. Let's figure out what we can do."

"There's nothing!"

Chloe surprised herself when she screamed the two words at her sister. But once they were out, she found it hard to reel them back in.

"Chloe, I—"

"I messed up. I failed you and Mom and myself. This is me now. I have to live with this and just…"

"But we can figure it out together, right? Look…I dig this role reversal and all, but I can't stand to see you beating yourself up like this."

"Not now. I can't deal with it right now. I have to figure some things out."

"Let me help, then."

Chloe felt suffocated. She also felt another outburst coming on, but she clenched her fists and was able to stamp it down. "Danielle," she said as slowly and as patiently as she could, "I appreciate the sentiment and I love you for being so concerned. But I need to handle this on my own for right now. The longer you pester and press in, the harder it's going to be. So please…for right now…can you just leave?"

Chloe watched as something in Danielle's expression shifted. It looked like disappointment. Or maybe it was something closer to sadness. Chloe couldn't tell and, quite frankly, she didn't care in that moment.

Danielle set her beer down on the coffee table—not yet even a quarter of the way empty—and got to her feet. "I want you to call me when you're done being distant."

"I'm not being distant."

"I don't know *what* you're being," Danielle said as she opened the door to leave. "But *distant* sounded better than *a bitch*."

Before Chloe could say anything in response, Danielle made her exit, closing the door behind her.

Chloe wished Danielle would have slammed the door. At least then there would have been some sort of feeling left, some sign that Danielle was just as mad as Chloe was. But there was only the soft click of the door closing and nothing more.

Chloe sat in the silence that followed for the rest of the afternoon and all she had to show for it the next day were more empty beer bottles in the trash can.

Chapter Two

On Sunday, Chloe found herself sitting in a visitor parking space outside of the DC Central Detention Facility. She looked at the building for a moment before getting out of the car, trying to figure out exactly why she was there.

She knew the answer, but it was a hard one to swallow. She was there because she missed Moulton. It was a truth she would never speak out loud, a sore spot that she was having trouble processing. But the plain and simple truth was that she needed someone to comfort her and ever since she'd moved to DC, she'd seen Moulton as that figure. Oddly enough, it was something she had not come to realize until after he had been sent to prison for his role in a financial fraud scheme.

At first, she'd thought she only missed him because of the physical intimacy—the need to be held by a man when she was feeling discouraged and lost. But when Danielle had left yesterday and Chloe had found herself desperate to talk to someone about what she was dealing with, she thought only of Moulton.

With one final push of motivation, Chloe got out of her car and walked through the front doors. She used her federal ID to get inside, signed in, and then sat in a small holding area as a guard was sent back to get Agent Moulton. The holding area was basically empty; apparently Sunday was not the most popular day to visit troubled loved ones in prison.

Less than five minutes later, Moulton appeared through the door in the back of the room. The room itself was set up like a small lounge of sorts. Chloe was sitting on a couch, which Moulton slowly approached. He looked at her with a skeptical smile, as if trying to size her up.

"You okay if I sit here?" he asked, uncertain.

"Yeah," she said, scooting over to allow him room on the couch.

"It's nice to see you," he said right away. "But I have to admit that it's also very unexpected."

"How are you being treated here?"

He rolled his eyes and sighed. "It's mostly guys like me. White collar crime stuff. I'm not ever really worried about getting jumped in the showers or beaten up in the exercise yard, if that's what you mean. But I don't even want to talk about that. How's work? Working on anything of interest?"

"No. They partnered me back up with Rhodes. She and I have been working this profiling project. A little boring at times, but it keeps us busy."

"You two getting along?"

"Better than the first time around, that's for sure."

He leaned in closer and once again gave her a skeptical look. "What brings you to these parts, Fine?"

"I wanted to see you."

He smiled. "That makes me feel much better than it should. But I don't buy it. Not completely anyway. What's up?"

She looked away from him, starting to feel embarrassed. Before turning back to him, she was finally able to squeak out something of an answer: "My father."

"Your father? The one who just popped back up in your life a few months ago? The one that spent most of the last twenty years or so in prison?"

"Yeah, that's the one."

"I thought you were happy about that, for the most part."

"I was. But then something else popped up. And then something else. There's just been this huge pile of crap that keeps getting added onto. And this last thing I discovered … I don't know. I think I just need someone not attached to him to give me an opinion."

"Maybe someone who worked closely with you before getting thrown in prison?"

"Maybe," she said, giving him a smile that felt a bit too flirty.

"Well, hearing the story would be the most interesting thing I've taken part in over the past two weeks or so. So let me hear it."

It took a few seconds for Chloe to find the courage to talk about such a personal issue but she knew it needed to be done. And as she started telling Moulton about Danielle's constant warnings about their father as well as the revelations discovered in the journal, she understood why she had refused to discuss it with Danielle; it was opening her up to vulnerability. And that was not a state that Danielle had ever seen her in.

Even as she told Moulton everything, she kept some of the more private details to herself—particularly when it came to memories pertaining to her mother's death. But getting out the bits she did was extremely helpful. She knew that at the core of it all, this was nothing more than a venting session. Be that as it may, it still felt like a weight had been lifted from her shoulders.

It helped that Moulton never questioned her or even made faces to indicate his true feelings on the matter. He knew what she needed; she just needed someone to listen—someone to maybe even offer some advice.

"I assume you've considered taking this to Johnson?" he asked when she was done.

"I have. I've thought about it a lot. But you know as well as I do that nothing would be done just because of a few journal entries written two decades ago. If anything, it would probably just clue him in. The moment police or FBI start questioning him, he'd know something was up."

"You think he'd run?" Moulton asked.

"I don't know. You have to remember…I don't know him all that well. He spent most of my life in prison."

"And what about you and your sister? Do you feel safe? You think he'd come after you?"

10

"Doubtful. He still sees me as his confidant. Although I'm sure he might figure something is up since I haven't returned his calls or texts. And I'm not answering the door when he comes by."

Moulton nodded, understanding. He was looking at her in a way that was slightly uncomfortable. It was the same thing she had seen in his eyes a month or so ago when they had nearly slept together. And God help her, she wanted to kiss him quite badly in that moment.

"You know what you have to do," he said. "I don't know if you came here hoping I'd back you up on it or what."

"I know."

"Then say it. Speak it out loud and make it real."

"I need to find out for myself. Not an official investigation, but just... keep tabs on him, I guess."

"You think that involves reaching back out to him?" Moulton asked. "Maybe just carrying on like normal, as if everything is the same as it was before you read those journal entries?"

"I just don't know."

A brief silence fell between them, which Moulton eventually ended with a sigh. "There are a lot of things I'm going to miss out on because of what I did," he said. "Too much stuff to really even think about, honestly. But one of the things I'm starting to truly regret is that I think you and I could have been pretty great."

"I'm trying *not* to think about that."

He nodded, looked into her eyes, and slowly leaned in. She felt herself being drawn toward him like a magnet, could even feel her lips starting to part to accept his kiss. But she turned her head at the last minute.

"Sorry. I can't. All this nonsense with my dad... the last thing I need is some weird strained relationship with a criminal."

He chuckled at this and rested his head playfully on her shoulder. "You're right," he said, pulling his head up and looking at her. "But hey... I call rights on being able to hit you up when I get out of here."

"And how long will that be?" Chloe asked.

"Officially a few years. But good behavior and some bureau loopholes ... no one is sure just yet. Could be as little as eight months."

"Yeah ... I'll give you first rights," she said.

"Something to look forward to ... that's good. Because this place sucks. The food, though ... better than I expected."

She was reminded of why she enjoyed his company. He had seamlessly transitioned the awkward talk of her father into something else. And he had done it without making her feel like a burden.

They sat on the couch for another fifteen minutes as Moulton described what life had been like for him over the past few weeks. He was taking it all with a grain of salt and had no qualms about fully admitting his guilt and remorse. It was good for Chloe to hear it—not just because she believed he truly was a good man deep down, but because it showed that people *were* capable of being honest.

And given the nightmare she could feel brewing between her, Danielle, and her father, being in the presence of any kind of honesty was hugely refreshing.

She took her leave forty minutes after she had gotten out of her car in the parking lot. Moulton had not tried to kiss her again, though she secretly wished he would. She left feeling oddly satisfied, feeling that she was finally moving forward after three weeks of feeling stagnant and stymied.

As she made the walk back across the parking lot, her phone rang. She grabbed it right away. It was probably Danielle or her father. If it was her father, she thought she might actually answer it this time and make up some excuse as to why she had been dodging his calls. She figured he'd accept just about any reason, given the fact that he had just suddenly reappeared in her life after almost twenty years.

But the number she saw on the display was neither her father's nor Danielle's. It was a line from the bureau. She cringed a bit as she answered it. A call on a Sunday was sure to set up a stressful Monday.

"This is Agent Fine," she answered.

"Fine, it's Johnson. Where are you right now?"

She actually had to bite back a small laugh before answering. "In town," she answered as vaguely as possible.

"I need you to visit a crime scene in Falls Church. Seems to be right in the area of your expertise. Wealthy neighborhood, murdered socialite-type."

"Today?"

"Yes, today. The body was discovered Friday morning. The police have done their part and are coming up blank."

"Just one body?"

"Yes. But we need an agent on it to ensure that it isn't linked to a similar case in that area last year."

"Sir...do you think Rhodes can handle it alone? I'm sort of dealing with some personal things."

There was a brief moment of silence on the other end. "Is someone dead? A loved one pass away?"

"No sir."

She knew that Johnson knew the scantest details about her father's history. She wondered if he was silently considering all of that on the other end.

"Sorry, Fine. You've spent three weeks in an office, putting a profile together. I want you out in the field. I want you and Rhodes both down in Falls Church within three hours. Two if you can manage it."

She opened her mouth to protest but stopped herself. She had no desire to be knee-deep in a murder investigation given everything she was dealing with. But at the same time, she knew that getting involved in a case might be exactly what she needed. It would not only distract her from the drama with her dad, but it might put her in the right frame of mind to figure out a way to bring down her father.

"Yes sir," she said. "I'll call Rhodes right away."

And just like that, she had her first active case in three weeks. The timing wasn't the best but who was she to argue? At the end of the day, she'd joined the bureau to help people in need—to help bring a sense of justice to a criminal system she had never fully trusted.

In light of all that had happened concerning her father in recent weeks—including her own misconceptions about him—it seemed almost fitting that it was this mindset that followed her as she got into her car and called up Agent Rhodes.

Chapter Three

I f Rhodes suspected that Chloe was dealing with personal issues, she made no mention of it as they rode out into Falls Church. In fact, she had not said anything about a change in Chloe's personality for the three weeks they had been working together on the profile project—trying to come up with a profile on a man believed to be leading the charge on a series of armed bank robberies in New York. Then again, Rhodes was something of a hard ass and kept to herself. Even when their partnership had hit a new level after Chloe had saved her life following a near-fatal gunshot wound, Rhodes showed no signs of wanting to know Chloe on a deeply personal level.

And that was perfectly fine with Chloe.

In fact, most of the drive from DC to Falls Church, Virginia, was covered in silence. Johnson had not given them much to go on; the details on the murder were practically nothing. All he'd told them was that the local deputy would be on the scene to debrief them when they arrived.

The closest they came to a meaningful conversation occurred just as they got off on the exit ramp to enter Falls Church. "You know much about this city?" Rhodes asked.

"A bit. Mostly upper class, I think. But this neighborhood we're headed to, if I remember correctly from a case study back in the academy, it's one of those areas that's rich mainly because of what they call *old money*."

"Ah, you mean rich people that are rich because mommy and daddy were rich and didn't have anything to do with the money after they died."

"Basically, yes."

Rhodes chuckled and looked out the window. "It seems to me that you and I have become the go-to agents on things like this. Well … you, anyway. How do you feel about that?"

It wasn't anything Chloe had really considered before. She simply shrugged and answered honestly: "I guess everyone needs a niche to specialize in."

Rhodes let it go after that. Chloe was doing her best to convey that she had no interest in small talk right now—trying to get the point across without being too rude. Apparently, it worked. They made it to the crime scene—a beautiful two-story home in an affluent neighborhood—without another word spoken between them. Most of the lots were either wooded or boasted huge backyards. The neighborhood itself was a bit removed from the more densely packed neighborhoods, giving each home a bit of space to breathe.

The presence of a single police car in the driveway seemed terribly out of place. It gave the residence an almost haunted feel after having seen so many of the other homes. It was like a blemish on the neighborhood.

They parked the car and walked up to the porch. The door was closed, so Chloe knocked, not wanting to be presumptuous by just walking in when there was an officer there waiting for them. Her knock was answered right away. The officer who opened the door looked to be in his early thirties. He was clean-shaven, quite plain looking, and appeared surprised to find two women on the other side of the door.

"We're Agents Fine and Rhodes," Chloe said. "We were sent to look into the murder of Jessie Fairchild."

The officer extended his hand and introduced himself. "Deputy Ed Nolan. I'm running the wrap-up on this. Come on in."

He ushered them inside, where Chloe discovered the house was larger inside than it had appeared outside. The foyer was nearly the size of the living room in Chloe's apartment and the ceilings were at least twelve feet over her head. The place felt as if it hadn't been lived in for quite some time, giving Chloe a creepy vibe.

"So what's the story here?" Chloe asked. "All we've been told is that we need to rule it out as connecting to a case from last year."

"What case is that?" Nolan asked.

"Three strangulation deaths about five miles away from here," Rhodes said. "All women, all between the ages of forty and sixty."

"Yeah, I think we'll be able to rule that out pretty quickly."

"Why is that?" Chloe asked.

"Well, the body has obviously been moved by now, but I can show you the pictures. Mrs. Fairchild wasn't killed by strangulation, although she had been strangled too. It was more like a slice to the throat...but in a weird way that I've never seen before."

He led them into the kitchen and grabbed a file folder from the bar. He used it to point up the stairs as he said, "The house cleaner discovered the body in the master bedroom upstairs. She went up while leaving the utility sink in the mudroom going. She obviously got a little sidetracked by finding the body, so much so that the utility sink overflowed."

"Let's go take a look at the bedroom, then," Chloe said.

Nolan nodded and took the lead. As they passed through, Chloe noticed that either the cleaning lady was exceptionally good at her job or the Fairchilds just naturally kept a clean house.

The upstairs hallway was just as impressive as the downstairs. A bookshelf stood at the end of the hall, built into the walls. There were four rooms along the hall, two of which were bedrooms, the third a secondary bathroom, and the fourth an office.

Nolan led them to the master bedroom. While the body had of course been moved, Chloe saw that the sheets had not been removed since the murder.

"The room is exactly as it was when the body was discovered?" Chloe asked.

"All we moved was the body," Nolan confirmed.

"Can you walk us through the details?"

He did just that as Chloe looked around the room with Rhodes. She listened to each detail, trying to play it all out in her head, imagining the scenes taking place in the room in which she currently stood.

"Rosa Ramirez, the house cleaner, discovered the body around eleven thirty in the morning. Police were on the scene just before noon. I was part of the initial party to respond to the call, so I was able to see everything in this folder firsthand. Jessie Fairchild's throat had been cut, but in a very strange and grisly fashion. While we *do* believe there was strangulation involved, the cutting was done with a very large diamond ring."

"You're sure about that?"

"Positive. Forensics confirmed it late yesterday. It was coated in blood and the jagged lines of the cut match the cut of the diamond. For what it's worth, her husband isn't sure if the ring belonged to his wife."

"Hold on," Rhodes said. "There's no way a diamond ring is big enough to cut that deep."

"We thought the same thing," Nolan said. "But the angle of the cut hit a vital artery and it also punctured the windpipe."

"Any motive?" Chloe asked.

"We originally assumed it was a home invasion or robbery. I'm sure you've noticed that this place is loaded with valuables." He pointed to the walk-in closet on the left side of the room and added: "There's a disgusting amount of jewelry in there. When we talked to the husband, he pointed out a necklace that's worth about thirty grand. And it wasn't in a safe, either. Just hanging there, on a plain old jewelry rack. There's also two cars in the garage, one of which costs about three years of my salary. A huge pool in the back, a spa-level hot tub. It's being humble to say the Fairchilds were loaded. And with them being new to the neighborhood, we assumed it was a robbery. But we can't find any evidence of that."

"Was *anything* taken?" Chloe asked.

"We had the husband do a run-through to look around, but he came up with nothing. He said he could not see where anything had been taken. Of course, he was distraught from having had his wife recently murdered so who knows how accurate of a search he did…"

"You said you thought there was some sort of strangulation involved," Rhodes said. "Do you know what she was strangled with?"

"We don't know for sure, but we think it was a fox stole—this fur wrap sort of thing. We found it tucked under the bed. Forensics says they're pretty sure both ends of it had recently been tightly gripped and pulled. The husband also said he couldn't remember the last time he'd ever seen her wearing it."

"What can you tell us about the Fairchilds?" Chloe asked. She was stepping toward the bed, looking at the dried bloodstains on the top sheet.

"They were new in town. Moved in about five weeks ago. There are still some boxes out in the garage that they hadn't even unpacked yet. The husband, Mark, is some kind of big-shot banker...something with finances and stocks. Jessie Fairchild dealt with social media...some kind of influencer for C-list celebrities. Instagram, Facebook, stuff like that. Moved here from Boston...the husband said it was because they were just getting tired of the big-city congestion."

"Where is the husband now?" Chloe asked.

"He went to some cabin out in the mountains with his brother. Left this morning, actually. He's um...well, he's a wreck. I mean, people take death different ways, I know. But this man...I watched him just sort of crumple and wither up, you know? It was the worst I'd ever seen."

"No fingerprints anywhere on the scene, I take it?" Chloe asked.

"None. We did find a single loose hair on that fox stole, though. It was blond, and Jessie Fairchild was a brunette. It's being tested as we speak...should know something pretty soon."

Chloe took a moment to take it all in. Because there was a strong indication of at least *some sort* of strangulation, she could not rule out a connection to the murders from a year ago. But the cut with the diamond ring told her this was something new...something different. She picked up the folder and nearly opened it up to start digging into it right then and there.

"You said you're in charge of wrapping the loose ends?"

"Yeah."

"Can we follow you to your precinct? I'd like to get a workstation set up."

"So you *do* think it's related to the strangulation murders from last year?" Nolan asked. It was clear that he had not been expecting this.

"I don't know for sure," Chloe said. "But what I do know is that a woman is dead—that she was killed in her own home—and we currently have no one in custody. So … let's get to work."

Nolan smiled at her go-get-'em attitude. He nodded and started back for the bedroom door, headed to the hall. "Let's get started then."

CHAPTER FOUR

Chloe opened up the folder on the Jessie Fairchild murder as soon as she was settled down at the precinct. Nolan had given them an office that had once belonged to an assistant deputy who had been let go as a result of cutbacks. Some of the former assistant deputy's belongings had been left behind, making Chloe feel out of place.

Still, she buckled down and pored over the information in the file. She was impressed with how well put together it all was. Apparently, Deputy Nolan had a knack for organization and details.

Beyond the basic police report, which included everything Nolan had already told them at the Fairchild residence, there were several pictures of Jessie Fairchild's body. She was fully dressed, on the bed. Her head was cocked to the left, her opened eyes staring in the direction of the pool of blood that had collected around her head. The most noticeable feature of her body, though, was the ragged laceration along the center of her neck.

The pictures must have been taken within several hours of the murder because most of the blood was still wet. She could see where it was starting to congeal, but it was still mostly fresh. The cut itself was quite brutal. It was jagged and gruesome, a straight line that looked almost as if it had been sawed into the flesh. Chloe could also see very slight indications that something had been wrapped around her neck, though it was hard to tell for certain from the photos. Without seeing the body, she'd have to take the word of the forensics team. But if what she *did* see was indeed where something had been wrapped around her neck, it would line up perfectly with the fox stole that she saw in one of the other pictures.

She also saw a picture of the diamond ring that had been used to make the cut. It was sitting on the bedside table; the killer had not made any attempts to clean it or hide it. As far as Chloe was concerned, this was the killer trying to send a message.

But what message?

"The ring is throwing me off," Rhodes said. "Why put it right there on the bedside table? Is he bragging? Maybe trying to tell us something?"

"I was just wondering the same thing. I wonder if the ring has any special meaning. Why *that* ring. It looks like one of those engagement/wedding ring combo deals."

"It also looks expensive as hell," Rhodes added.

"It's got to be symbolic in some way. You don't just accidentally place a blood-soaked diamond ring on a nightstand after using it to kill someone."

"So you think it's the killer trying to tell us something?"

"It might be. It could also—"

She was interrupted by the ringing of her phone. She pulled it out, assuming it would be Johnson to make sure they had arrived. But when she saw **DAD** on the display, she cringed a bit. A flare of anger went spiraling through her, leaving bits of fear in its wake.

She ignored the call and placed her phone face down on the desk. When she returned her attention to the folder in front of her, it was hard to get back on track.

"You okay?" Rhodes asked.

"Yeah, why?"

"Well, you just looked at your phone like it called you a slut or something."

Chloe shrugged, hating the passive feel of it. "Just personal stuff."

Rhodes nodded, clearly not wanting to engage in anything deep. "Yeah, personal stuff can certainly suck."

As Chloe continued to try getting refocused on the folder, there was a knock at the door. When it opened, she saw Deputy Nolan's face peeking in. When he opened it wider, she saw another man behind him. He looked much older and wore one of those thick gray moustaches that always reminded Chloe of a walrus.

"Agents," Nolan said, "this is Chief Clifton."

Clifton came into the office and looked at both of them, giving nods of appreciation. He looked at the folder, currently opened on the desk and revealing one of the photos of the gory cut along Jessie Fairchild's neck, and quickly looked away.

Chloe and Rhodes ran through a quick series of introductions as Nolan entered behind Chief Clifton, closing the door behind him.

"Was Deputy Nolan able to get you everything you needed?" Clifton asked.

"Absolutely," Chloe answered. "He was very accommodating."

"Is there anything else we can get for you?"

"Well, being that it was such a large house, I'm assuming there was a security system. Any evidence of that?"

"Yes, actually," Nolan said. "The husband gave us the code so we could reset it after leaving the house."

"And he never got any sort of alerts that the alarms had been tripped?"

"None."

"Can we get some sort of report on that?" Rhodes asked.

Nolan and Clifton nodded in unison. "I'll get in touch with the security company," Nolan said.

"Also, we'd obviously want to speak with the husband," Chloe said. "Deputy, you said he was in the mountains somewhere with his brother, right? Any idea when he's coming back?"

"No idea. He didn't say."

"I'd really like him to be here, in town," Chloe said.

"You suspect him?"

"Not necessarily. But he is the man closest to the victim." She did not put an accusatory tone into her voice, though she did find

BLAKE PIERCE

it irresponsible that the police had simply allowed the husband to leave.

"I'll get him on the phone, too. He might actually be very accommodating. If he knows the FBI is on this and it will help catch the killer, I think he might get down here pretty quickly, actually."

"One last thing," Chloe said. "I know you said the Fairchilds are new to the area. But do either of you happen to know if Jessie Fairchild had any enemies? Any calls or complaints about her and her husband, or maybe from them about someone else?"

"No, nothing like that," Clifton said. "But that neighborhood…hell, that whole area…it's sort of a mess. We do get calls from time to time. Jealous wives trying to catch their husbands in affairs that don't exist, snooty homeowners trying to get their neighbors in trouble because their dog shit in their yard. People in that neighborhood think far too highly of themselves."

"Forgive me for asking, but why are you telling us this?" Rhodes asked.

"Because while I would not go so far as to say that Jessie Fairchild had enemies, I can almost guarantee you that she had women in the neighborhood that were at least *envious*. It's a very snotty neighborhood. I know that's not the best thing for a police chief to say, but it's the sad truth of the matter."

"Well, that could potentially mean there's a deep pool of potential leads," Chloe said. "If these are the types of women you're insinuating, there might be quite a bit of gossip. Maybe they already know some things and can lead us in the right direction."

Clifton chuckled under his breath and shrugged. "I wish you the best of luck with that."

Chloe knew where he was coming from but was irritated by the unhelpful nature of the comment. "For now, I'd like the contact information of the cleaning lady who discovered the body."

"We've already spoken to her at length," Clifton said. "You're welcome to just look over our notes." He was not necessarily being defensive, but wanted to make sure she knew that they weren't totally inept. She wondered if that had anything to do with him

24

realizing that they probably should not have let the husband leave town so soon after the murder.

"All the same, I think I'd like to speak with her personally."

Clifton folded his arms but nodded. "I'll see that you get that information promptly," he said. He gave a quick smile before saying: "It was nice meeting you, Agents." With that, he opened the door and headed out.

Nolan cringed and said, "He gets like that. Especially the few times we've worked with the bureau or other outside agencies. Control issues...just between the three of us."

Chloe made a zipping gesture across her mouth. "I get it. Now...if we can get the cleaning lady's information, I'd like to meet with her before it gets too late."

CHAPTER FIVE

Rosa Ramirez lived in an apartment just on the cusp of the nicer edge of the downtown district. When she took the call from Nolan, she seemed quite eager to help Chloe and Rhodes. When they arrived at her apartment at 4:30, it was clear that she had straightened up her place just for them. She even had coffee and graham crackers set out on her coffee table as snacks.

"Ms. Ramirez," Chloe said, "how long had you been working for the Fairchilds? As I understand it, they had only been in town for about five weeks."

"That's right. I responded to a help wanted ad I saw online. This was about a week before they even moved out here. They wanted everything set up and ready to go when they moved in. That included a house cleaner. I even stepped in to help them unpack some of their things."

"Did they seem grateful for the help?"

"Yes. It was clear that they weren't exactly used to people so willing to help out."

Chloe helped herself to the coffee even though she usually tried to limit her caffeine intake. She wanted Rosa to feel at ease; a comfortable witness or lead was often more prone to stumble across truths they may not even realize they had.

"Were there ever any cross words between you and the Fairchilds?" Rhodes asked.

"No, not a single one. Honestly, I even went in asking for a rate a little over what I typically ask for and there weren't even any negotiations. Neither of them ever spoke a negative or cross word to me."

"What about the two of them?" Chloe asked. "Did you ever see them arguing?"

"No. I've been trying to think about that myself but I can't think of a single time. Now, keep in mind that for the five weeks I worked for them, I only saw them together two different times. Mark was usually off on business."

"Any idea where he would go on these business trips?"

"All over. But I think it was primarily on the east coast. Boston, DC, New York."

"Do you know if Jessie resented him for it?"

"If she did, she hid it well. She kept herself busy. Like *really* busy. I don't know that she gave herself time to even really notice that her husband was gone."

"Busy how?" Rhodes asked.

"Well, the neighborhood they live in is filled with prominent people. Or, if I'm being honest, people who *think* they're prominent. Jessie was already trying to find her place in that scene. She was sort of dipping her toes in all of the social circles…garden clubs, fundraisers, looking into helping organize local gala events, that sort of thing."

"Did she officially join one of those things?"

"Not that I'm aware of."

"Ms. Ramirez, I'm sure you understand that I need to ask you where you were for the earlier part of the day that you discovered Jessie Fairchild's body."

"Yes, I know," she said, letting out a little sigh. "It was Friday. And on Fridays, I take the morning to myself. Sometimes I just sleep in and catch up on a few TV shows I watch. Other times, I get errands done. But this past Friday, I was actually at the library for part of the morning."

"Did anyone see you? Would there be anyone that can confirm that?"

"Yes. I was emptying out some of my old boxes in storage. I donated a ton of old paperback books to the Friends of the Library.

I wheeled them in on one of the library's little dollies and even helped the assistant librarian shelve them."

"So you remember what time this might have been?"

"Sure. I got there just after ten thirty, I think. I was out of there around eleven or a little after. Then I drove out to the Fairchilds' house."

"Did you stop anywhere along the way."

"I did. I stopped at Wendy's to grab lunch."

"And when you arrived at the house … you saw nothing strange or out of the ordinary?"

"Nothing at all. The first strange thing I saw was Jessie, on the bed in her running clothes."

"We were told by the police that her husband was here in town … not on business. Do you know if there is any truth to that?"

"I think so. Usually they let me know when Mark is going to be away. But as far as I know, he was at the local office on Friday. I got there right around eleven thirty … which means he had probably been gone about three or four hours by the time I got there."

"Ms. Ramirez," Rhodes said, "do you feel there's any chance at all that Mark might have killed her?"

Rosa shook her head confidently. "No. I mean, I know nothing is impossible, but I really doubt it. He's a nice guy. And very playful and kind with her. They're both in their early fifties … the kind of couple that still holds hands. I even saw him playfully smack her on the butt one time, like two young newlyweds. They seemed very happy."

Chloe let this all sink in. She was confident that Rosa had nothing to do with Jessie Fairchild's murder. She'd have the local PD follow up on the alibis she'd just given, but she felt it would be wasted effort.

"Thank you for your time," Chloe said, finishing up her coffee with a long gulp. She handed Rosa one of her business cards as she headed for the door. "Please contact me if you think of anything else."

Rosa nodded as she walked them to the door. "There *is* one thing that comes to mind," she said.

"What's that?"

"The ring on the nightstand … the one used to cut into her neck. It had no business being there. Jessie was sort of a neat freak—it's why she had a housekeeper even though she kept a mostly clean house. I had never seen jewelry just sitting out."

Chloe nodded, as she had been hung up on that, too. The ring being there not only served as some sort of message from the killer, but it also proved that the murder was likely not related to wealth or a botched burglary. The ring was an expensive one and had been used as nothing more than a crude weapon. Even though the killer had it in their hands at one point, they'd had no interest in ever stealing it.

And that alone spoke volumes about the killer.

Now, Chloe thought, *all I have to do is translate the killer's message.*

Chapter Six

It was just after five when Chloe and Rhodes left Rosa's apartment. It was only about a forty-minute drive from where they had parked back to DC. Chloe considered this a big plus, as it eliminated the need for checking into a motel. The can of worms it opened up, though, was that it was hard to tell when to call it a day.

"Should we head to the library to check out Rosa's alibi?" Rhodes asked as Chloe pulled out of the apartment complex parking lot.

"I thought about that, but it's Sunday afternoon. It's doubtful the library would even be open. I was thinking I'd like to find out where that ring came from. See if we can maybe figure out who last wore it. If the husband doesn't recall it even belonging to his wife..."

Rhodes opened her mouth to respond but the chirping of Chloe's cell phone stopped her. Chloe answered right away, hoping for a lead on what was looking to be a slow and grinding Sunday afternoon.

"This is Agent Fine," she answered.

"Agent Fine, this is Deputy Nolan. I thought you'd want to know that I was able to get in touch with Mark Fairchild, the husband. He's due to come by the station around eight tonight. He and his brother are headed back home to take care of funeral arrangements, insurance paperwork, and things of that nature."

"And he knows the FBI is looking into things now?"

"He does. He seemed pleased, and eager to speak with you."

"I'll see you at nine, then," Chloe said, ending the call exactly as she had hoped: with another source of information lined up. When the information came to you rather than having to hunt it all down, it tended to make for a quick and easy case.

Chloe just hoped things continued at this pace.

It was clear from first glance that Mark Fairchild had not been sleeping well. From his appearance alone, Chloe was willing to bet he had not slept a wink since being told his wife had been killed. There were dark circles around his eyes—eyes that seemed to be staring at nothing at all while managing to look rapidly around the small conference room, as if trying to take everything in. His hair was disheveled and a growth of thin stubble covered the lower half of his face.

Still, he looked somewhat centered and determined. He sat partially slouched in a chair, holding a cup of coffee that Nolan had given him, but not sipping from it. His brother was standing in the corner, looking just as tired but carefully watching over his grief-stricken sibling.

Chloe knew that the coming conversation could be difficult. Grieving people who were clearly tired, still dealing with the idea of their recent loss, could be precarious. They could either talk endlessly, often in circles, or lose control of their emotion within just a handful of seconds. So she knew she'd have to choose the leading questions carefully, giving him the feeling that he was in control.

"Mr. Fairchild, I'd like you to walk me through Friday morning. Include every detail you can, no matter how small or trivial you feel it might be."

He nodded, but looked clearly uncomfortable. "Everything," he said with a sleepy grin that looked rather forced. "Well … my alarm went off for work. I hit snooze and when I did, Jessie came to me and snuggled up … sort of a tradition we've had since we were dating. It was Friday and had been a good week for both of us so snuggling led to sex. She enjoyed it in the morning; it was really nothing out of the ordinary."

Chloe felt awkward as she watched his face go through several emotions as he recalled the start to the morning. She gave him a moment as he paused, clearly making sure that he was going to be able to get through it.

"So I hopped in the shower while she answered some work e-mails. I got out of the shower and she was brushing her teeth. There was some small talk. As I got dressed for work, Jessie put on her running clothes—the same ones she was wearing when …"

He trailed off here, taking in a deep breath. He looked to his brother, who gave Mark an encouraging nod. Mark returned the nod and then started again, his voice a bit shaky.

"We went downstairs. She had a smoothie and I had a cup of coffee. She never drank coffee before her run. She said it played hell on her stomach. She walked me to the door, I remember that. She usually does that, just to kiss me goodbye. She was fiddling with her airpods, cueing up whatever podcast she'd been listening to so she could listen to it on her run. We kissed, I got in the car, and that was it. That was the last time I saw her alive."

"What time do you believe it was when you left the house?" Chloe asked.

"I don't know an exact time, but it was somewhere between seven fifty-five and eight-oh-five, I'd guess. Certainly no later than that."

"So we're looking at a three-, three-and-a-half-hour window," Rhodes said.

"Mr. Fairchild, had you and your wife made friends yet? Anyone who had come over a few times since you'd moved in?"

"No. Just acquaintances. There had been people in the house, sure. When a new family moves into the neighborhood, people come over with pies and cookies and things like that, you know? But I think the only person who had ever stepped foot in the house that was more than just a welcome-to-the-neighborhood kind of thing was the housekeeper. Oh, and the plumber. We had an issue with the garbage disposal on the first week."

"I want to also talk about the ring found on the bedside table," Chloe said. "I understand that you can't confirm whether or not it belonged to your wife?"

"That's right. It didn't look familiar, but that's not unusual. Jessie never really wore jewelry…just her wedding ring. That may seem silly because the closet is full of jewelry. But Jessie sort of collected jewelry the way some women go crazy with shoes or purses. When her mother passed away six or seven years ago, Jessie got all of her mom's jewelry. Necklaces, rings, these awful-looking earrings. But it put a fire under Jessie. She started to collect that sort of stuff."

"Do you recall how many rings came to Jessie through her mother?"

"No. I remember it was mostly in a safety deposit box. Some of it was, anyway. I do know that she received a small box with some necklaces and rings. There had to be at least ten rings in that box."

"So you'd say there's a decent chance the ring found at the scene was one of the ones that came from her mother."

"Probably. But that's the thing…she kept them in the closet. Whoever did that…"

He stopped here, as if the mere mention of what had been done with the ring had frozen him. He sucked in a breath and shook his head, determined to go on.

"Whoever did it," he continued, "must have known where to look for it."

"That or they simply got lucky and figured out where expensive jewelry might be kept."

"True," Mark said.

"And the week leading up to Friday…was there anything particularly off about your wife?"

"No. I've been wondering that myself…wondering if I missed anything. But I swear…she seemed perfectly fine."

"We understand that Jessie had started to try to get involved in local groups and organizations," Rhodes said. "Do you happen to know which ones?"

"She talked a lot about Kid's Cove, this non-profit that raises money for kids that have trouble paying for school lunches and things like that. There was another one…some garden club or something like that. I'm pretty sure I know where she kept names and numbers of all of those people, if you'd like to see it."

"We have a copy of that already," Nolan said.

Mark nodded, rolling his eyes. "That's right. I swear…these last three days just sort of all blur together."

"I'm sure," Chloe said. "Mr. Fairchild, thank you for your time. Please…go home and get some sleep. And I ask that you stay in town for the foreseeable future just in case we have more questions."

"Certainly."

He got up and gave a halfhearted wave as he and his brother exited the room. Nolan followed them out, closing the door behind him.

"What do you think?" Rhodes asked Chloe when they were alone again.

"I think even if Mark Fairchild *did* have something worth telling us, he probably wouldn't remember. I think he's telling the truth about that morning, though. His cheeks flushed when he mentioned the sex. And those pauses he took…he was legitimately fighting back tears and a potential sobbing fit."

"Yeah, I noticed that, too."

"Still, it paints an interesting picture, doesn't it? A new wealthy couple comes to town. The husband has a job that keeps them solidly in the upper class. And they seem to get targeted right away…less than five full weeks after they've moved in."

"You think they were running from something?" Rhodes asked. "You think they maybe moved to Falls Church to get away from something in Boston?"

"Could be. I'd like to know as much as I can about his job. Maybe get a peek at the Fairchilds' financial information and criminal records. Maye even talk to Mark's employer if I have to."

"And I think we need to also check the security company," Rhodes said. "I find it odd that no alarm was tripped. It makes me think Jessie Fairchild willingly let in the person that killed her."

As they mulled all of this over, the conference room door opened and Nolan came back in. He looked drained from having been in the presence of a man who had been so heartbroken and distressed.

"Nolan, what do we know about Mr. Fairchild's job?" Chloe asked.

"He's a standard broker. From what he tells me, he just got lucky with a few deals early in his career. It led him to some high-profile clients becoming very happy with him. He was quite humble about it, but he told us that he brought in a little over six million last year."

"And it's all on the up and up?"

"As far as we can tell. We haven't done a deep, through check into their finances yet, or into his tax returns from last year. We told him it might come down to that before it was all said and done. He seemed a little offended, but gave us his blessing. Even gave us a few numbers to call where he works if we need help."

"So in other words, he's not hiding anything when it comes to money."

"That's right. Clean as a whistle from what we can tell. But I'll probably still call some of the numbers he gave, just to say it's been done."

"I didn't see any note of a criminal record in your files, either," Rhodes added.

"Yeah. Both of the Fairchilds have clean records. Nothing. Not even a speeding ticket."

Chloe looked to the file folder on the table in front of her, suppressing a frown. True, the case seemed to already be veering far away from the strangulation deaths the year before. But there was still a death that had gone unsolved.

She stared at the folder, as if willing it to give her the answers. She had basically memorized what was inside; it told the story of Jessie Fairchild's murder in forms, reports, notes, and crime scene photos.

And for right now, the story seemed to be very open-ended.

CHAPTER SEVEN

Chloe had forgotten how useful car rides with a partner could be. They left Falls Church at 8:42 that night and headed back to DC but they made use of those forty minutes. Before they were even out of Falls Church, Rhodes had managed to get a manager from Intel Security on the phone. Intel was the brand of security system the Fairchilds had set up on their property. Chloe listened to the conversation as she headed through the night back home.

She smiled here and there, realizing just how good Rhodes was when it came to dealing with people. Chloe had noticed how Rhodes only asked questions during investigations when she had a good one to ask. She wasn't much for asking one hundred questions and hoping one might stick. She was the same way on the phone when speaking with Intel Security. She polite and cordial, but there was no pussyfooting around what she needed. As such, though, it was hard for Chloe to keep up with the information she was getting, as she was only hearing Rhodes's short-and-to-the-point side of the conversation.

Several minutes later, when the call was over, Rhodes filled her in. Here, Chloe realized another of Rhodes's strengths. She was a copious note-taker and often didn't even need to take the notes at all. The woman's mind was like a lockbox when it came to details.

"Okay, so the gentleman I spoke with said there is no sign that the alarm was sounded last Friday morning," Rhodes said. "He also pulled up their data timeline and said he didn't see where the alarm had been disengaged at all. It wasn't cut off by one of the Fairchilds at any point."

"Did he give you details on how it works?"

"Yeah. The alarm kicks on when the door is opened with force. Opening with a key automatically disengages the alarm. When the door is opened from the inside, it is also disengaged. The only time the alarm would kick on other than someone essentially picking the lock or kicking the door open is if the door is left standing open for more than twenty seconds."

"In the few weeks they've been there, were there any instances of the alarm going off?"

"He said there were two notes on their account. Both came from the first week they were living there. Intel gives courtesy calls when the alarms are triggered. On both of the calls, Mark Fairchild said they'd neglected to fully close the door while bringing in boxes `and furniture as they were moving in."

"What about windows? Does the alarm work for windows as well?"

"According to what I was just told, any time a window is opened from the outside, the system has to be deactivated. They gave an example of spring cleaning—making sure the windows and frames are all cleaned. If someone planned to do that sort of cleaning, they should kill the alarm first."

"But you're saying there were no suspicious alarm triggers over the last week or so, right?"

"Not a single one."

"So in other words," Chloe said, "whoever killed Jessie Fairchild did not break in. They were allowed to come inside."

"Seems that way."

The car went quiet as they both pondered this. Chloe knew where they needed to start looking next. So far, all they truly knew about Jessie Fairchild was that ever since she and Mark had moved to Falls Church, she had been looking into how to get involved in local groups and organizations. New to town, neither she nor Mark had any real friends—and that meant most of the people they spoke to would be unreliable.

But she also thought about a question that had come up earlier. Had the Fairchilds perhaps left their home in Boston because they had been running from something? If the investigation ended up taking them into the lives of the Fairchilds all the way back in Boston, this seemingly simple murder case could become a lot more convoluted.

"No friends, no local family," Rhodes said out loud as they neared DC. "A sister in Boston, both parents deceased. If this thing takes us into Boston ..."

Chloe grinned, pleased with how the two of them were starting to think along the same lines, at the same speed. "Well, wasn't there a note somewhere in the file about a relative of Mark's? Someone who lives right outside of Falls Church?"

"Yeah, his uncle. But from what I gather, he's on some kind of trip. A vacation, I think."

She answered it with the sort of nonchalance that made Chloe think Rhodes felt the same way about that potential lead as she did—that it wouldn't come to much anyway.

Closing in on home, Chloe slowly allowed herself to slip into more personal thoughts. She strongly considered calling Danielle to apologize for her behavior yesterday. But those kinds of conversations with Danielle typically turned into a rather long discussion, and she did not have the stamina for that.

They returned to bureau headquarters, swapped out the bureau car with their own, and parted ways. Chloe once more thought about Danielle before she left; she even considered driving out to Danielle's new place—an apartment she had rented just twenty minutes away after moving so her ex-boyfriend had no idea where she was living.

In the end, she decided against it. She knew she and Danielle would be okay—that sometimes, it just took some extra time for both of them to cool down. Still ... she had an hour before she needed to ramp down for the night. And with things at a stand-still on the Fairchild case until morning, there was one other thing she could do that came to mind. The thought seemed to flip her insides, making her feel slightly sick, but the impulse was there and she acted on it almost immediately.

She pulled out into the street and pointed her car toward her father's apartment.

❧   ❧   ❧

She had no intention of actually seeing him, let alone speaking to him. But she needed to prove to herself that she was capable of even driving past his place. It would have to happen at some point if she wanted to check up on him so she may as well get over her nerves as soon as possible.

His apartment was less than half an hour from bureau head-quarters, and less than twenty minutes away from her apartment coming in from another direction. It was 10:08 when she cruised into the parking lot. His place wasn't so much an apartment as a townhouse … the kind of home that was directly attached to another, and then another, in an apartment complex style. She knew the car he drove—a used Ford Focus—and it was parked directly in front of his place. A light was on, visible through the main window.

She paused without parking, peering at that light and wonder-ing what he was doing. Was he just watching TV? Reading, perhaps? She wondered if, when he cut that light out and got ready for bed, visions from his past flooded his mind … his daughters, his dead wife. She wondered if the torture and torment he had put them all through kept him awake some nights.

She certainly hoped so.

Anger started to rise up in her. It rushed through her, hot like injected venom, until she realized that her hands were gripping the steering wheel tight enough to show the whites of her knuckles.

Maybe I should just go in right now, she thought. *Knock on his door and lay it all out. Let him know I know what he did … that I read Mom's diary …*

It was compelling enough to make her heart feel like it might burst out of her chest. A pleasant little rush of adrenaline plowed through her bloodstream as she considered it.

But of course, she could not go there. Not yet …

Chloe found the closest empty parking spot and used it to turn around. She headed for home, not realizing until she came to the first stoplight that she still had the steering wheel in a death grip.

CHAPTER EIGHT

It had been quite eye-opening for Danielle to realize that once her last relationship had ended, she found herself unemployed again. The bartending gig and the too-good-to-be-true dreams of running her own bar had been enough to float her through life for a few months but here she was again, without a man and without any sort of meaningful job.

She'd always done a good job of masking her contempt for shit jobs, but this one was particularly difficult. She was bartending at a strip club—only the management was adamant about not calling it a "strip club." They preferred either just "club" or "gentlemen's lounge." As far as Danielle was concerned, it didn't matter what you called it. The fact of the matter was, there was currently a woman on stage, rhythmically shaking her ass in a man's face to the beat of some shitty Bruno Mars song.

She finished making the mojito a customer had just ordered (*seriously, who orders a mojito at a strip club?*) and handed it to him. He was about fifty and when he took the drink, he made no effort to hide the fact that he was checking out her boobs. He smiled at her and sipped from his drink, his eyes never leaving her chest.

"You should be up on the stage, you know?" he said. Finally, he looked to her eyes, maybe so she could see the seriousness in his drunken gaze.

"Wow. I haven't heard that one before. What a unique pick-up line."

Confused, the guy eventually sneered at her and then moved away from the bar and took a seat closer to the stage.

Yes, she'd had more than a dozen guys clearly baffled that she was behind the bar and not on the stage. Her manager was one of them. And while Danielle had endured enough demeaning jobs in the past, she drew the line at taking her clothes off for drunk men so they could slip fives and tens down her thong.

She knew this was just a temporary job. It *had* to be. She wasn't sure what she would do to get out of this, though. Maybe she'd finally finish college. She had another year and a half left…and even though she'd be almost thirty by the time she graduated, it would at least be *something*.

Not that the perks of this job were anything to sneeze at. She'd had the job for a month, working four nights out of the week. On her second week, she'd garnered more than seven hundred dollars in tips alone. But it was the atmosphere and the feel of the place. Even when the goth girls came out and danced to music Danielle actually enjoyed, she felt the need to get out as quickly as she could.

Besides…sometimes when the dancers came to the bar or when she happened to run into them backstage, Danielle was always surprised to see that they didn't look miserable. And when she saw them folding those fifties and hundreds up as if they were just handling napkins, the thought of getting up on stage wasn't *all that* terrible.

That, more than anything, was why she wanted out of this place as quickly as possible.

She looked up and down the bar and noticed the crowd was thinning out. There were five people at the bar, three of whom—a male and two females—looked to be huddled very tightly, perhaps making plans to close out their Sunday night. Danielle checked her watch and was surprised to see that it was 11:50. Another hour and she could go home…she could go home and sleep until noon—something she had missed over the course of the last year or so as she had tried to become a more responsible adult. A responsible adult who had been far too dependent on a man, but a responsible adult nonetheless.

She started wiping down the drip trays under the taps and checking the liquor bottles to get an updated inventory sheet for her manager. She was in the middle of the tequila row when she heard her name called out from behind her.

"Hey, Danielle."

It was a male voice. She tried to place it. Only a few guys that frequented this place had bothered to remember her name. She frowned, not in the mood for lighthearted flirting, even if it *did* mean a pretty nice tip.

She turned around, putting on her best agreeable face. But her expression froze when she saw the man sitting at the bar.

It was her father. He not only looked out of place sitting right there in front of her—but the sight of him in a strip club was surreal. To his credit, though, he *did* look incredibly uncomfortable.

The word *dad* formed on the tip of her tongue, but she swallowed it down. She wouldn't give him the satisfaction of calling him that to his face. Instead, the most obvious question came out of her mouth first.

"What the hell are you doing here?"

"I came by to see you," he said. He leaned forward, as if trying to distance himself as far as possible from the two topless women on the stage twenty-five feet behind him.

"Let me try another question," Danielle said. "How did you know I worked here?"

He frowned and nodded to the liquor bottles behind her. "Can I get a whiskey first?"

Acting as quickly as she could, Danielle grabbed a glass and filled it halfway with the cheapest whiskey the place had. She all but slammed it down in front of him. The entire process took less than ten seconds.

"There. Whiskey. Now…speak."

"I'm not proud of it," he said, "but I followed you."

"From where? How do you even know where I live?"

He drained the whiskey in one full chug, grimacing as it went down. He slid the glass to her and gave her a nod to fill it up. Danielle took the glass and slid it to the side.

"Answer the question," she snapped.

"I don't know where you live. I was driving by Chloe's place last week. Went up and knocked on her door because she won't answer my calls or texts. As I came out of the building and got in my car, I saw you. You were heading into the building and I—"

He stopped here, glancing over his shoulder as a new song came on. Behind him, the same two girls started dancing and gyrating against one another to a newer deplorable excuse for a rock song.

"Can we talk somewhere else?" he asked.

"No. I'm working."

"Five minutes, Danielle. That's all I want."

She nearly refused him, but then realized that he had answers she wanted. How did he know she worked here? What else did he know about her? And why the hell was he here in the first place?"

"Hold on," she said.

She went to the door at the left edge of the bar and opened it. To the right, the dancer who had just come off of the stage was walking up a flight of stairs to the changing room. To the left, a small hallway led to three other rooms—an employee bathroom, an office, and a small break room for the girls.

Her manager was standing in the doorway to his office, speaking with another dancer and the backup DJ. He saw Danielle poking her head out the door, dropped what he was discussing, and came walking to her. It wasn't that she was all that important—she was simply the only bartender on duty; she had been since nine o'clock that night, as Sundays tended to be relatively slow.

"Everything okay?" he asked.

"No. Look … can you man the bar for like ten minutes? My fucking father decided to show up. And we don't have a great—"

"Say no more," he said with a smile. "I understand parent issues more than I care to admit."

"Thanks," she said. She doubted the bit about parents was true. He was always nice to her, probably because he was always trying to recruit her as a dancer.

He came out and stood behind the bar, allowing Danielle to lift the little employee door on the side. She didn't even look at her father as she passed by him. She simply said, "Come on already," and headed for the exit. She nodded to the security guard at the back entrance and he stepped aside to let them pass through.

The exit door led them outside to the back of the building where employees parked and came out to smoke. It was also the area where handsy patrons got tossed after security hauled them off.

"So you were stalking Chloe and what now?" Danielle asked, not seeing the point in wasting any time.

"I wasn't stalking. I was concerned."

"You saw me go in and then what?"

"I waited. I had no idea where you lived. Honestly, when I came to DC, I had no idea you were even living here."

"I wasn't then." She nearly added that she was now but didn't see the point in sharing that bit of information with him.

"Anyway, I waited. I didn't think it would be smart to try speaking to both of you at the same time."

"Smart decision."

"So I waited. You came out about half an hour later and I followed you. You came directly here. I almost followed you in but realized that might be weird. I thought maybe you were … well, dancing and—anyway, I got the nerve up to sort of look and was relieved when I found that you were just behind the bar."

"And you waited a week to surprise me?"

"I figured I'd come in when it was slow."

"What for? What could you possibly have to tell me? Or are you going to ask me for money the same way you asked Chloe?"

"No, nothing like that. I just … well, I worry about you. I worry about both of you."

"We've done fine without you for the last twenty years or so."

"I can see that. But … I need you to tell me what I can do to fix things. I thought Chloe and I were fine and now all of a sudden, she's gone dark on me. And then there's you. You and I have never really been close …"

"And do you know why?" she barked. God, she wanted him to say *no*. She wanted to throw it all in his face. All the things she had witnessed him do to their mother. Even the way she had never felt safe around him as a result—and how he had used that to essentially rule over her as a sick kind of authority figure.

"Yes, I know. And I'm sorry, Danielle. I truly am. I just want things better. I missed your childhood...both of you. I just want. A family again. And I need you and your sister to tell me it's not too late."

She believed him; as much as it pissed her off to admit it, she believed the bastard. Really, what reason did he have to seek them out...especially after Chloe blew the lid off of his affair with Ruthanne Carwile? Maybe he was being sincere.

For a moment, Danielle thought about what life would be like with some semblance of family. Chloe and her distant father, all coming around her again. She had never truly known what family was like. What might it be like to step into the future with the support of a family around her?

"I just don't know," she said. "There's been a lot of hurt. Chloe...she always fought for you. She refused to see the side of you that I always saw...the side that you really never ever tried to hide from me."

"I know, I—"

"But that's changed now. After she saw the diary, things changed for Chloe."

By the time she finished the sentence, Danielle knew that she may have screwed up. He had no idea they had seen the diary. As far as he knew, she and Chloe were both ignorant to just how bad things had gotten—to just how scared their mother had truly been in the days before she had been killed.

She saw a flicker of surprise in his face, but only for a moment. But it was all it took to see that he had not been expecting this.

"What diary?" he asked. His voice was low, almost in a hiss.

"We found one of Mom's diaries."

"And what makes you think either of you should have it? Or read it?"

"What is it, Dad? Afraid we might find something we shouldn't?"

An expression crossed his face then, one that made her think that, just for a moment, he might hit her. But it flittered away quickly and she could tell that he was trying to pass it off—to pretend he wasn't bothered by it.

But he did his best to pass it off. He looked away from her for a moment, nodding. "You understand ... I had to try."

"I don't understand. But then again, I didn't make choices that caused me to be taken away from my family for nearly two decades."

"This was a mistake," he said. "But ... have you been here all night?"

"Yes, why?"

"I thought ... well, I thought I saw you riding by my place tonight."

"No. Not at all."

He thought about this for a moment before shrugging. "I saw someone ride by. Caught the briefest glimpse of their face as they turned around in one of the streetlights. I could have sworn it was you."

"Hell no. Not me.

"Chloe maybe?"

"Right now, there would have been a better chance of it *having* been me."

He considered this for a moment and then started for the door again. "I'm going to go. I shouldn't have come."

"Go around the building. Don't go back through. Spare me *some* awkwardness for the rest of the night, please."

He hung his head, as if doing his best to milk some sympathy from her. He did as she asked, walking to the other side of the building and disappearing into the shadows. Danielle watched him go as she slowly made her way back to the exit door. Yet as she reached for the handle, her mind kept returning back to one particular moment of the awkward conversation.

While she may have slipped up in revealing that they had seen their mother's diary, it had been telling. He had perhaps revealed a bit too much about himself.

Because unless she was totally reading too much into things, it seemed to Danielle that the moment she had accidentally mentioned the diary, her father had suddenly been in a rush to leave.

CHAPTER NINE

The following morning, Chloe and Rhodes swapped positions from the previous night. Rhodes made the drive from DC to Falls Church while Chloe made several calls. The first call was made at 7:30, to Deputy Nolan. When he answered, he did so with the sort of vibrancy in his voice that made Chloe assume he was a morning person.

"Good morning, Agent Fine. Headed back our way this morning?"

"I am, actually. And I was hoping you could put a list together for me. Between what you've determined on your own and what Mark Fairchild has offered, could you get me a list of all of the organizations and groups Jessie Fairchild was speaking with since they arrived in Falls Church?"

"Can do. I'll text it to you within fifteen minutes."

It was the sort of morning that got Chloe's blood pumping. She'd had a well-rested night, a decent breakfast, and now, before eight o'clock, had a list of things to get done coming her way. It was a day filled with promise and potential—and while she usually wasn't one to buy into the power of positive thinking, feeling so hopeful this early in the morning was always a plus.

Nolan texted the list as promised less than ten minutes later. As Rhodes closed the gap to Falls Church, Chloe started to make calls. There weren't too many names on the list, but finding the right contact information within each of the groups and clubs took more work that she had been expecting.

By the time they arrived at the police station, it was 8:12 and they had come up with a plan of attack. Chloe watched as Rhodes typed down her own to-do list on her phone, as they had decided they would cover more ground by splitting up. When it came to interviewing multiple people—especially within what seemed like an atypical suburban neighborhood—it was often the most effective way to get things done.

"Want to meet back up for lunch?" Rhodes asked as Chloe got out of the car. One of them would need to use a loaner from the PD, and Chloe had volunteered. A chance of pace and scenery—even something as minor as a mode of transportation—sometimes got her thinking differently, seeing things from a different perspective.

"Yeah, we can do that. Hopefully we'll have enough notes to start comparing."

Rhodes gave a nod and then pulled away, leaving Chloe to head into the station. Nolan was sitting at a desk in the bullpen area, speaking on the phone with someone. He saw Chloe come in, gave her a smile, and then tossed a set of keys to her. He then gave a little nod, his eyes lingering a bit longer than necessary, and looked away.

Chloe turned away to hide her grin. She was sure Nolan had no interest in her, but it was always nice to be appreciated in a non-verbal (and, more importantly, a non-creepy manner). She headed back outside and to the lot along the side of the station where the patrol cars were parked. The tag on the keys Nolan had lobbed to her was labeled with the number 6. She was pleased to find that it was to one of two unmarked Dodge Chargers—probably the second or third most common unmarked police car next to the Crown Vic.

Chloe got into the car, pulled up the address to the first meeting she had scheduled while on the way into town this morning, and headed out to start what she hoped would be a productive day.

The first woman she was scheduled to meet with was Candace Derringer. Ironically, she lived just three houses down from the Fairchild residence. Candace was the director of a local charity called Feed the World, an organization that worked to assist the city government with making sure the homeless in the area had somewhere to get a warm meal.

On the phone, Candace had seemed a little too enthusiastic about meeting with Chloe, sounding as if she was having a friend over for coffee and bagels rather than an FBI agent. As Chloe pulled into the driveway, she saw that Candace Derringer had perhaps been thinking *exactly* that; she was sitting on the large wraparound porch, perched at an ornate patio table with a carafe and a plate sitting in front of her.

Chloe walked up the porch steps, trying her best not to seem put off by Candace's little setup. Candace smiled at her, a smile that lit up her forty-something face to the extent that it made her look closer to thirty.

"Agent Fine?" she asked.

"That's me," Chloe said.

"Good, good. Have a seat. The coffee is fresh and the bagels, regrettably, are plain."

"That's fine. I think I'll just have some coffee if that's okay."

"Sure," Candace said, instantly pouring the coffee into one of the available cups sitting on the table.

"Ms. Derringer, I hope you understand that I have several people to speak with today. I appreciate the spread here, but I really can't stay long."

Candace smiled and gave a polite nod. "Oh, I wouldn't expect you to, Agent Fine. This is just something I do a few times a week. Sitting out here, inviting up anyone that might be walking by. Most people in this neighborhood are quite close and either work from home or are retired. So you never know who might stop by on any given morning."

"That's a great segue to why I wanted to speak with you," Chloe said as she doctored her coffee up with sugar and creamer that were also sitting on the table. "I wanted to ask you about the Fairchilds."

"I figured that's what this was about. That poor woman…"

"Did you know Jessie Fairchild very well?"

50

"Not *very* well, no. But she sat in that chair you're in right now on two occasions. She was looking for ways to volunteer with Feed the World. She seemed very genuine about it, but we never really got her started."

"Any reason why?"

"She never really followed up. We'd set up an appointment for me to take her to the little headquarters we have but she would always ask to have it pushed back."

"Did she give any reason for pushing the appointments back?"

"She'd just say something had come up. But I think—and please forgive me for making ill assumptions of the dead—I think she just wanted to *appear* like she wanted to be involved."

"Why do you say that?"

Candace looked visibly uncomfortable, peering into her coffee cup. "Well, keep in mind that I did not know her all that well, so this is all based on a general perception of her ... but I feel that she was faking it. And I can't say I blame her. New to the neighborhood, in her late forties, early fifties ... you have this need to fit in, you know? I think she was desperate to fit in. But it didn't really work."

"What do you mean?"

"Well ... if I'm being honest, you're going to be hard pressed to find anyone in this neighborhood—or in the little groups and organizations some of us are part of—that got a good impression of Mrs. Fairchild."

Chloe was a bit surprised. She had not been expecting this level of honesty. From her experience, most women from these sorts of neighborhoods were hesitant to speak badly of someone, even not behind their backs. Those conversations were usually saved for sharing with spouses and close friends.

"Do you know why?"

"I've only heard it from a few people, but I think moving here sort of backfired on the Fairchilds. They are extremely wealthy, as I'm sure you know. Most of the people in this neighborhood have a good amount of money. But the Fairchilds were different. You can just look at them and the way they carry themselves... they're *spoiled*. Do you know what I'm trying to say?"

"So it's a jealousy thing?"

Candace smirked a bit, as if slightly offended. "No, not really. Maybe way down deep for some people. But I think it's more of not being used to having someone look down on you. Jessie did that and I don't think she even knew it. It rubbed people the wrong way, you know?"

"When you had these little morning meetings with her, did she ever say anything that upset you?"

"Not really. Like I said... she never made anyone feel small on purpose. But when you can't talk about anything but the three weeks you and your husband spent in Paris two years ago or the weekend away in Maui... it gets a little old."

"I don't suppose you ever took note of the jewelry she wore, did you?"

Candace took a moment to think it over and then shook her head. "No. The only jewelry I know she wore regularly was her wedding ring. I stared at it for a while the first time she was over here. It's gorgeous... and another soft-spoken example of how loaded the Fairchilds are. That ring... it had to have cost at least fifteen to twenty grand."

Chloe mulled this over as she sipped from her coffee. This was what she had feared the most: trying to get any useful information out of socialite women who likely saw anyone wealthier than them as a threat of some kind. Sure, Candace was doing her best not to come off as such, but the fact that she kept bringing up the Fairchilds' wealth spoke volumes.

"But what I'm hearing you say," Chloe said, "is that you never heard her out and out insult anyone?"

"No."

"Not even in a gossipy wort of way?"

"No. And that's the irritating thing. I think she was a nice person when you got right down to it. It was just the way she carried herself."

"And what about her husband, Mark?"

"I don't know. I never met him. But I spoke to a few others here in the neighborhood that met him—a few that spoke to him at length. From what I hear, they're both genuinely nice people."

"Can you think of anyone who might have had some sort of altercation with Jessie? Maye just a few cross words?"

"Well, there's a woman who sets up the schedules for the Chamber of Commerce seasonal events, particularly the fundraising side of things. Her name is Lauren Engle. She met with Jessie a few times, too. Sort of the same story as with me. They met a few times to see how Jessie could volunteer but nothing ever came of it. Lauren seemed to *really* not care for Jessie. I don't know that anything ever transpired between them, but Lauren said she just had this gut reaction to Jessie."

"But she wouldn't say what it was about?"

"No. Again…look, I know women like us might be known as gossiping busybodies and it's slightly unfair. But for the most part, we're innocent. Lauren never told me one specific thing. She just said she really didn't care for Jessie Fairchild and would never give me a reason."

"That didn't seem odd to you?" Chloe asked.

Candace shrugged as she sipped from her coffee. "Maybe a little."

"Do you know where I might find Lauren right now?"

"She works at the city courthouse…an assistant for the Recreational Department. It's Monday, so I'm sure you'll find her there."

"Great. Thanks so much for the time…and the coffee."

"Of course," Candace said. She seemed a little shocked that their time together was over. To Chloe, it looked as if she was thinking hard about something, like there might be something she was trying to decide on.

Chloe reached into her inner pocket and retrieved one of her business cards. She set it down among the coffee and bagels, Candace watching on closely.

"Please call me if you think of anything else or hear anything."

"I will," Candace said, taking up the card.

Chloe turned and left, wondering what it was about Candace that seemed a little off. She doubted Candace had been one hundred percent honest. If she'd had some sort of disdain for Jessie Fairchild, she probably wouldn't come out and admit to it.

She got into her borrowed Charger and pulled up directions to the city courthouse. By the time she pulled out onto the street, feeling the morning already starting to get away from her, she wished she'd reconsidered and taken one of Candace Derringer's bagels.

Lauren Engle was a mousy little woman who did not look at all surprised to have a visitor from the FBI. Even when Chloe showed the woman her badge, Lauren did not seem fazed. It made her wonder if Candace had tipped her off. And if that was the case, *why?*

Lauren sat at a desk in a quiet office. Somewhere in a room behind them, two people were talking. Other than that, Monday morning in the Falls Church Office of Events and Recreational Planning was dead.

"Can I ask what this is about?" Lauren asked. She had a deep southern accent that was so deep it almost sounded fake, like a bad actor trying it out.

"I'm investigating the murder of Jessie Fairchild. And since she had not yet made many friendships in town, I'm forced to speak to just about anyone who had any significant conversations with her."

She could have easily stopped after mentioning Jessie's name; the look of scorn on Lauren's face said enough.

"Well, I didn't know her very well personally."

"Oh, I know. But I spoke with Candace Derringer and she said you had spoken with Jessie about potentially helping with Chamber of Commerce seasonal events."

"Yes, that's true. But that never happened."

Chloe felt bad for wanting to cringe every time the woman talked. The accent was incredibly annoying. But the more she spoke, the more Chloe became certain it was *not* an act. This was the real thing.

"Any reason?"

"She wasn't interested. I got the feeling she was just testing the waters of several local organizations, charities, groups, things like that. I think she was just looking for that right fit."

"It was implied that you had a distaste for her. Any reason?"

A brief look of shock went across Lauren's face, but she quickly got it under control. Chloe figured this was an internal struggle for her. Lauren had clearly not expected Candace to tell others just how strongly she had disliked Jessie Fairchild—especially not a federal agent.

"You could tell her nice attitude and cheerful smile were all just sort of fake. She wanted to fit in, wanted to pop right into the social circles after coming to a new town. I had a brief lunch with her and at first thought she was genuine. But we started cracking jokes, sort of easing the tension of meeting someone new, you know? I'm sure it was a slip-up on her part, but she referred to other people in her own neighborhood as 'small-time.' I thought it was just really tacky, you know?"

"Did she flaunt her wealth in front of you?"

"Not directly. It was weird … she didn't *have* to. She carried herself in a way that made it clear she thought she was better than you. Sort of snobby, but in a very vague sort of way."

"Do you know if she'd made any enemies in town?"

"I don't have any idea. She was just … God, this sounds terrible, but she was easy to dislike, you know? But I'm sure Candace told you all about that."

Chloe kept to herself the fact that Candace had, in fact, *not* told her such a thing. She only nodded, trying to think of a way to steer the conversation. Sadly, she felt that it was pretty much already over. She didn't necessarily suspect either Lauren or Candace of any sort of foul play, but it was clear that they were both trying to save face. They did not want to admit to the federal agent that they thought the recently murdered woman in town had been a stuck-up bitch.

"You know," Lauren said, an idea suddenly coming to her. "I wouldn't call it an enemy by any means, but there *was* this gala event two weekends ago. There was a silent auction and one of the big ticket items was this really nice boat. Jessie outbid another woman—a woman who typically wins those sorts of things. There aren't many in this area that flaunt their wealth, but this woman did from time to time."

"And were there words between the two?" Chloe asked.

"No. But you could feel the chill in the room, you know? It was very uncomfortable. There was a change in the air … and when you get around a lot of wealthy people, change isn't usually accepted very well."

"Do you have this other woman's name and contact information?"

"Her name is Rachel Dobbs. I don't have her contact information available, but I could get it for you."

"That would be helpful."

As Lauren went looking through a few files on her computer, Chloe noted just how relieved she seemed to have passed the burden of answering questions about Jessie Fairchild onto someone else.

It left Chloe with the uncertainty of whether or not Lauren was relieved because her own feelings toward the deceased weren't the best or because she was keeping pertinent information from her. Honestly, she assumed the former because the deeper she got into this, the more she was coming to realize that seeking information from wealthy women who hardly knew the victim was not going to amount to much.

And if that was the case, she was going to have to find a different approach.

CHAPTER TEN

Chloe and Rhodes met at a quaint little sandwich shop for lunch. By nothing more than the look on her partner's face, Chloe could tell that Rhodes hadn't been very successful this morning, either. They sat down at a table by a window, Rhodes wasting no time getting to the point.

"Well, I hope your morning was more productive than mine." She scooped up one of the menus on the table and started to scan it with only the slightest bit of interest.

"Depends," Chloe said. "How many jealous white women did *you* speak to?"

"Three."

"I only spoke with two. So it looks like yours was more productive than mine. What did you find?"

"Just that no one in any of these little social circles cared much for Jessie Fairchild. And it wasn't even that anyone was rally jealous of her, per se...just sort of..."

"*Unfamiliar* is the word that comes to mind," Chloe said. "It's not only that the Fairchilds were new, but it's that they were incredibly wealthy. It made people uneasy. It shook up their little status quo."

"Yeah, that's a good way to explain it. That, and I got the impression that no one wanted to be the one to actually come out and admit that *they* didn't like Jessie. They tried to pass it off on others."

"Yeah, I got some of that, too," Chloe said.

A waitress came by to take their orders, leaving them both to ruminate on the little bit they had already discussed.

"The only real lead I got was a woman who got outbid by Jessie Fairchild at some sort of silent auction," Chloe said.

"I heard that story, too," Rhodes said. "I got it from one of the women at the Garden Club—which, for the record, sounds like an abysmally boring club. I got her contact number. I think she's the next stop for us."

"I got it, too. Great minds thinking alike and all that. Did you get any intel on the husband?" Chloe asked. "Any indications if he was liked or not?"

"No one I spoke with seemed to have any opinion on him. It was all about Jessie and how she seemed to flaunt her wealth in this passive kind of way. How about you?"

"Nope, not a thing. But I also got some of those complaints of how Jessie seemed to sort of wave her wealth around. Again, though . . . it was almost like no one wanted to speak ill of her."

They continued to compare notes but for the most part, it was retreading over familiar ground. At this point, they could only go over points they had already covered, things that were filed away in the police files on the case.

Their lunch came and they ate quickly. Somehow, noon had already come and this day, which had seemed to full of potential four hours ago, was starting to feel like it was getting away from them.

Finding Rachel Dobbs was easy, as she worked out of her home. She was heavily involved in the selling and promoting of essential oils as alternative medicines—a trend that was apparently getting very popular on her side of the city. When Chloe first heard what Rachel did as a means of employment, she had pictured a bored stay at home wife, selling a bottle of lemongrass or lavender here and there. But when Rachel Dobbs invited them into her home and then into her office, Chloe saw that this was very far from the truth.

Rachel had boxes upon boxes of the oils stacked up against her far wall. Over each stack of boxes, there was a small dry erase board on the wall with quantities, names, and other information.

"You look busy," Chloe commented as she sat down on the love-seat on the other side of the office.

Rachel, forty-eight and dressed as if she were about to head out for cocktails rather than just working out of her home, smiled. She sat on the edge of her large oak desk and looked to the boxes.

"Yeah, allergies are getting bad this time of year in this neck of the woods," she explained. "It's one of my busiest times of the year."

"And does your husband work as well?"

Rachel chuckled, nodding. "Of course. I mean, I do well with the oils, but Bradley is the breadwinner. He's a proposal strategist for privately funded groups out of DC and Richmond. He tinkers with military contracts here and there as well."

"Did he ever get the chance to meet either of the Fairchilds?" Rhodes asked.

Rachel frowned and looked down at her well-manicured hands. "He did. At the gala you mentioned on the phone. Now, you said on the phone you wanted to talk to me about the night of the gala specifically. If you don't mind my asking, what exactly did you hear?"

"Nothing bad," Chloe said. "We just gathered that it came as something of a surprise that Jessie Fairchild outbid you on a boat."

"She did. But if I do say so myself, I took it with a dash of grace. I know it may seem like Bradley and I are spoiled because of our success, but I'm not spoiled."

"And I'm not hearing that you are. Not at all. But we have it on the authority of two different witnesses that things felt awkward afterwards. And it's also been implied that you simply did not like Jessie Fairchild. Was it primarily because of the auction?"

"No, not at all. I had run into her a few times as she tried to find ways to get involved with community projects and organizations. And I wish I had something nicer to say, but I just didn't like her from the start. And I don't know why. It's just that thing where sometimes you know right away that you and another person just aren't going to get along. I felt that about Jessie from the start. And I am pretty certain she felt the same way about me."

"Why do you say that?" Chloe asked. "Was she ever rude to you?"

"Not in any blatant way, no."

"And did you see her with any regularity?"

"No. I take a spin class at the gym and she came to that two times. But no one really gelled with her and she stepped out."

"Did you ever speak to her in the class?"

"Just surface-level stuff. The weather, the traffic, how we liked the class. Things like that."

Chloe nodded as her cell phone vibrated in her pocket. She checked it and saw that it was Deputy Nolan. "Excuse me, please," she said.

She stepped out of the office, into the hallway. The walls were adorned with multiple pictures, all of what Chloe assumed were Rachel's family. She answered the call, hoping that Nolan was going to have a new lead for her.

"Hey, Nolan. What's up?"

"So, I looked a bit deeper into Rachel Dobbs after you called and filled me in. She got a clean record, as does her husband. The only place her name came up on a database search was when someone attempted to break into their house six years ago. But there is *one* thing I found that was interesting. It seems she's involved in a spin class at Crunch Fitness, one of those trendy little gyms here in town."

"Yeah, she was just talking about that. She said Jessie Fairchild took it a few times and then bailed."

"Well, I called around and spoke with the instructor. Seems that after the second class Jessie Fairchild attended, the instructor overheard a pretty catty conversation between Rachel Dobbs and some of the other women. Part of that conversation involved Dobbs saying, and I quote, *God, I could just kill that Boston bitch*. The instructor also said she was pretty sure some sort of boat was mentioned."

"That's interesting," Chloe said.

"Yeah, I thought you might want to know."

Chloe thanked Nolan and ended the call. She took a moment to weigh her options before she walked back into the office. Sure, that conversation wasn't enough to arrest her, but it *was* enough to warrant suspicion. She also knew that with women like Rachel Dobbs, they often became a different kind of person when they were taken out of their natural environment.

She made her decision and walked back into the office. She waited to Dobbs to finish answering a questions Rhodes had asked about the night of the gala. When she was finished giving a vague and non-helpful answer, Chloe stepped forward two steps—just enough to seem a bit intimidating.

"Mrs. Dobbs, I just received a call that shed some new light on this … particularly on your exchanges with and concerning Jessie Fairchild. I'd like for you to come with us to the station to answer some additional questions."

"Absolutely not."

"With all due respect, I wasn't asking. You can either come down with us now, peacefully and helpfully—we'll even let you drive your own car while we follow you—or we can escort you out. I'm sure your neighbors would love to jump on their phones and spread *that* story."

"I'm not a criminal! And I would certainly never *kill* anyone."

"I'm not saying either one of those is true," Chloe said, keeping her voice calm. "But the sooner you come along with us, the sooner this will be over. If you've done nothing wrong, you have nothing to worry about."

Rachel scowled, standing up from her desk and moving back and forth from one foot to the other. She looked as if she didn't know how to properly express the amount of anger coursing through her.

"Do you know what this will do to my reputation?"

"Whatever it is," Rhodes said, "I'm sure it won't be nearly as bad as us escorting you into a police car with handcuffs on your wrists."

"Fine," Rachel said, seething.

"You know the way to the police station?" Chloe asked.

"Yes."

"Then you lead the way and we'll follow."

Rachel walked right between Chloe and Rhodes on her way out of the office. There was so much anger and hatred in the woman's expression and even her posture that Chloe could feel it in the air as she passed. While she knew better than to equate that anger into guilt, she *had* dealt with enough people to know that the next hour or so was going to be a bumpy one.

CHAPTER ELEVEN

The anger Rachel had shown while in her home office had simmered down several notches by the time she was seated at the interrogation table in the Falls Church police station. There was still some rage in her, sure, but it was joined by anxiety and a good dash of fear. The result, Chloe saw as she and Rhodes entered the room, was a slight trembling in Rachel's arms and a nervous twitching in the right corner of her mouth.

She had not been cuffed to the table, as she was not considered a threat. The glare she gave the two agents as Rhodes closed the door behind them, though, suggested she might very well be capable of some sort of danger.

"This is embarrassing," Rachel said. "It's insulting ... to think ..."

"To think what?" Chloe said. "That we might expect you to explain yourself?"

"I have absolutely nothing to explain."

"We hear from your spin class instructor that might not be the case. Seems you have something of a habit of talking trash about people behind their backs."

She seemed confused—almost interested at first—but then realization dawned on her. Rachel sat back in her chair, arms crossed, looking at both of them as if they were absolutely insane.

"Is *that* what this is all about? Because I made some stupid comment to other women after a spin class?"

"So you do remember the comment we're referencing?" Chloe asked.

"Yes. And it was stupid and mean-spirited."

"Could you repeat it here, for us?"

"Are you serious?"

Chloe only nodded. She, too, crossed her arms and she stepped closer to the table. Rachel cringed a little at the closeness and relaxed her posture a bit.

"Look, it was nothing serious…just frustration coming out. We were just chatting and, I'll admit, maybe getting a little mean. And I might have said something about wanting to kill her. But it was an empty threat. It was stupid."

"We're told the words you used were 'I could just kill that Boston bitch.' Does that sound about right?"

"Yes. It was mean and stupid. And I would have never said it if I knew she was going to actually be murdered."

"What happened between the two of you to make you say such a thing anyway?" Rhodes asked.

"Nothing happened. We never spoke a cross word to one another. But there was tension there…unspoken tension. We just didn't like one another and the night at the gala sort of bumped it to a new level."

"What about the gala?" Rhodes asked. "Earlier, you said it really wasn't that big of a deal."

"It wasn't. It was just…"

"You'd been unseated," Chloe said. "You were used to winning these things, tossing your wealth around. And now someone comes to town with more wealth to toss around—someone that didn't know you felt *you* had earned that spot."

"That's not fair," Rachel spat.

"Fair or not, it seems like the truth. And it pissed you off bad enough to make that very stupid comment."

"So for making such a comment, I'm what…a suspect?"

"Not at all. Not yet, anyway. Can you confirm where you were last Friday morning?"

"Yes, actually. I had breakfast with a dear friend of mine. It's a Friday custom…breakfast with her before spin class. But I missed spin class this week. I had a chiropractor appointment."

"How long did all of that take?"

"I met my friend for breakfast at eight thirty. Spin class starts at nine thirty and ends at ten fifteen. I was back home around eleven thirty or so, give or take a few minutes."

"And there are people that can back all of this up?" Rhodes asked.

"Yes!"

Rachel snapped the last comment, nearly shouting it. It was clear that she was getting frustrated—not just because she was not accustomed to being treated in such a way, but because they were really drilling her. Chloe knew that it was time to let up; such specific details over the course of a single morning, especially when concerning a doctor's visit, would be fairly bulletproof.

Chloe took a step back and uncrossed her arms. "If you'll leave the name and contact information of the friend you had breakfast with as well as your chiropractor, you're free to go."

"Unbelievable," Rachel muttered as she pulled out her cell phone. But despite the anger, Chloe could also see relief washing over the woman's face.

As she got up from her chair, Rachel seemed bothered by something. She took only two steps toward the door before she sighed deeply and looked directly at Chloe.

"Did anyone mention Gwen to you?"

"Gwen? No ... no one has mentioned anyone named Gwen. Who is that?"

"I hate to even say anything. It's not my place and—"

The ringing of Chloe's cell phone interrupted her. She almost ignored it completely but felt she had to at least check it. If it was Danielle, she wanted to know. If it was maybe even Moulton, she wanted to know as soon as possible.

The caller ID read **DC Police**. It was a tag she had given for any number coming in from any Washington DC police units or directories. It had saved her a whole lot of confusion and back and forth phone tag situations when she'd been asked to work with them.

"Hold that thought," she told Rachel as she stepped quickly out of the room.

She answered the phone, anxious to get back to Rachel and hear about this Gwen character. "This is Agent Fine," she said.

"Agent Fine, hi. This is Officer Alice Henley with the DC Police. I wanted to let you know that I'm standing in front of your apartment right now. The door looks like it's been kicked in and the place is sort of a wreck inside. Looks like someone broke in."

"Oh my God. How long ago … do you know?"

"We got the call from your neighbor about half an hour ago … said they heard when the door was kicked in."

"Thanks. I'll be right there."

She opened the interrogation room door, poking her head in and looking straight at Rhodes. "I've got a bit of a personal emergency to handle back home. Can you hang here and finish this up?"

"Sure. Everything okay?"

"I don't know. I'll keep you posted."

Rhodes only nodded, obviously a little taken aback at the abrupt shift in the case. Chloe gave her an apologetic look as she closed the door and hurried down the hallway toward the front door.

She tried to think of a reason someone might break into her apartment. Hers was no different from those of the other residents around her. She didn't own anything particularly expensive and, honestly, knowingly breaking into the apartment of a federal agent was just about the dumbest thing a criminal could do.

Unless…

Unless it was my father … or Danielle …

Neither option made sense but somehow, the first one felt right.

My father … the journal …

By the time Chloe reached the parking lot, she was sprinting for her car.

CHAPTER TWELVE

Dusk had settled over the nation's capital by the time Chloe pulled her car into the parking lot in front of her building. The officer she had spoken with assured her that there would be a policeman on the scene when she arrived. Sure enough, when she went running up the stairs and down the second floor hallway to her apartment, there was a female police officer waiting for her.

"Agent Fine?" she asked.

"Yeah."

"I'm Officer Henley. Sorry to meet you under these circumstances."

Chloe only gave a perfunctory nod as she pushed open her door. She looked at the hinges and saw where they showed signs of recent stress; one of them had been knocked slightly askew, the screw holding it in bent and slightly popped out. The chain lock had been snapped, the longer half hanging from the slide bolted to the frame.

While the apartment was indeed in a ruined state, it wasn't as bad as Chloe had been envisioning it on the way home from Falls Church. A few of the kitchen cabinets had been left open. The little end table by the couch in the living room had been overturned. Every single door on the small entertainment center had been left open; DVDs and assorted cables and odds and ends were strewn all over the floor.

But the TV was still there (not that anyone would want to steal it, as it was at least ten years old) and her MacBook was still sitting on the little desk in the corner.

Someone came in looking for something very specific, she thought. And again, her inclination was to assume it had been her father, looking for her mother's diary.

Her heart dropped in her chest as she stepped through the living area and into her bedroom. She was barely aware of Officer Henley following her, pausing at the doorway.

"You notice they didn't take anything valuable?" Henley asked.

"I did."

"Any idea who might have done this?"

"No," she lied. The last thing she wanted was to accuse her father and get their drama wrapped up in legal proceedings, no matter how trivial. Besides…this was more of a personal matter. Bringing rules and laws into it would only complicate it. While Chloe was aware that this was a dangerous state of mind to take for a federal agent, she also felt that her father had fooled her for far too long. Maybe he was expecting it to become a big, legal thing. So, in that regard, Chloe sensed that it would be better to keep the entire ordeal between them a very quiet and personal matter.

Chloe looked to her bedside table and saw exactly what she had expected to see. The drawer on her bedside table was open. There were few personal keepsake items there, all tossed around. But the diary, which she had placed in the drawer late one night after the last time she had read some of its pages, was gone.

She was not surprised, but it still stung.

"Well, I guess you know the drill," Henley said. "We'll dust for prints, but that's about all we can do for now. I spoke with your neighbor. She said she heard someone kicking at what she thought was just the wall at first, but then heard the door get kicked in. She was too afraid to come out on her own, so she just called the police. I got here as soon as I could with my partner—a little less than twelve minutes after the call—but by then, whoever broke in was gone."

"Well, I appreciate your efforts."

"Can you see where anything has been taken? Anything at all?"

"Not from first glance, no." She hated lying so blatantly to a police officer but she didn't see how she had much of a choice. "So Mrs. Tasker, my neighbor ... she didn't see *anything*?"

"No. She said she stayed inside the entire time."

"I can't say I blame her," Chloe said. "I think I'm good for now."

"We have a team coming to dust for prints. Will you be here for the next little bit?"

"I don't know," she said. She was already thinking about why her father might take the diary. She had read everything in it and knew of all of his evils ... knew just how badly he had treated her mother. Perhaps he simply wanted it so that it could not be used against him in the future.

But would he really be so stupid? she wondered. *Somehow, he knew I had the diary. But if he's taken it, surely he knows I'll figure it was him.*

She also considered that it could have been Danielle. Maybe she had changed her mind and was reluctant to let her have it. But if that were the case, Danielle would just tell her. She didn't mind an argument or two when it came to getting her way.

Her father, on the other hand ...

"Agent Fine?"

Chloe realized she had gotten so lost in her own thoughts that she hadn't heard the last few things Officer Henley had said to her.

"Sorry ... just processing it all. What did you say?"

"I said to just call the station if there's anything we can help you with."

"Of course. Thanks, Officer."

Henley gave her a perplexed look as she made her way back to the recently kicked-in door. Chloe wondered if she was *that* obvious. Did Henley suspect that she knew more than she was letting on? If so, she said absolutely nothing about it as she left the apartment.

Chloe took a moment to mentally put things in order. The hell of it was that she knew her father was not a stupid man. He could have come in here and subtly looked around for the diary. Sure, he would have been in a burry after kicking the door down, but leaving drawers and cabinets open … making a mess in a few places … that was just sloppy.

And Chloe couldn't help but wonder if he had done it on purpose. Was he trying to send her a message?

And if so, what was it?

CHAPTER THIRTEEN

Chloe waited another hour before she headed back out. Night had completely fallen and she had managed to get her apartment in at least some semblance of order following the break-in. When she stepped back out into the parking lot at 8:21, she took a calming breath of the night air as she got into her car.

She could feel the structure of her personal life crumbling around her. It had been a foundation that had been fairly sturdy for most of her adult life. But then her father had come back into the picture. When Danielle had become a part of her life again, the structure had wobbled a bit. But now that her father was back, the foundation was rotting out. And for the first time in her life, she was starting to understand that he was indeed the cause of it ... that he was nothing but trouble, as Danielle had been trying to tell her for the last several months.

Back in her car, Chloe started the engine. Before pulling out into traffic, though, she pulled her Glock from its holster. She studied it for a moment and strongly considered taking it back inside. She stared at it for a moment and shook her head, returning it to her side holster.

She could be smart. She could be sensible and professional.

Repeating those two things in her head, Chloe pulled out of the parking lot and once again headed in the direction of her father's townhouse.

❧ ❧ ❧

Chloe was able to find a parking spot three spaces down from her father's door. She sat in her car for a while, looking in that direction. The same light she had seen on last night was shining again. As she was driving by, she thought she'd also seen the flickering light of a television set against the walls.

She knew what she wanted to do but it made her feel immature. And she knew if Director Johnson found out about it, she'd get a stern lecture.

So I guess I'd better be careful, she thought to herself.

She got out of the car, making sure her jacket was covering her side holster. She looked around the lot and the small expanse of lawn that sat in front of the row of townhouses. There were twelve in all, with a large parking lot breaking up the lawn before another two took over on the other side. Chloe did a quick check of the area and saw that the lawn and sidewalk in front of her father's row was empty. Three teens sat on small porch on the other side of the parking lot, but they were too enamored with something on a phone, the screen glowing bright into their faces, to even notice that Chloe was there.

She walked as casually as she could to the end of the sidewalk in front of her, walking to the right so it would take her directly in front of her father's apartment. As she passed she once again glanced through the window but saw only the light still on and the TV glowing from the left side of the window frame.

She passed by and came to the end of the row of townhouses. She then quickly darted to the left, hiding behind the last of the townhouses. There was another stretch of lawn here, mostly taken up by a strip of air conditioning units. Beyond those, there was a small row of city recycling bins. The reach of the streetlights diminished along this side before giving up completely, leaving the last few recycling bins hidden in utter darkness.

Chloe looked around the corner when she came to the end of the building. She, like the last few bins, was perfectly concealed by the darkness. She found herself looking at the back stoops of each of the townhouses she had just walked by. They were all identical: a small porch with a short set of stairs down to a small shared yard. The yard was bordered by a badly managed flower garden and a few towering trees, used simply to block the sight of another identical set of townhouses on the other side.

Along the back side of the complex, two back porch lights were on. But from what Chloe could see, there was no one out and about. She counted down four porches from where she stood, singling out her father's back porch. She wanted to keep some degree of stealth about her, but at the same time, she wasn't too worried about someone else living in the complex spotting her as she snuck through the darkness to her father's back door.

Still, there was some speed to her step as she walked across the grass. She kept close to the porches, making it harder for anyone who might be looking out to see her. She couldn't help but feel a little foolish, trying to sneak up on someone who would probably be happy to see her.

Well, he might have been happy to see me three hours ago, she thought. *But being that he broke into my apartment, it's probably a different story now.*

She made it to her father's back porch—the fifth one down—without being spotted. She didn't even give herself time to change her mind; she quietly walked up the back porch steps and approached the door.

She was a little surprised at how well the vantage point of the window in the back door worked out for her. The kitchen was off to the right. The door was situated directly against the left wall, giving a straight view of the small hallway that connected the kitchen to the rest of the townhouse. Because the lower floor was so small, she was able to see the single opened space just beyond the kitchen. There was no wall or bar area to separate the two; it was an open floor plan, giving her a clear view into the living room.

Her father was sitting in a recliner, watching television. The sight of him sent a spike of hatred and fear through her. The fear made her feel powerless, but she understood it. This was not only her father, but a man who had somehow had her thinking he had been something of a victim for his entire life. He had lied to her, fooled her... and here he was, after having broken into her apartment, sitting in his recliner and watching TV as if there was nothing amiss.

You don't know for sure he broke into your apartment.

Sure, it was a possibility. But given what she did for a living, it was not hard to come to the conclusion that it had been him who broke into her place. Who the hell else would break into her apartment and steal nothing more than some old diary penned by her mother? She was not at all surprised to see that he was not reading it. Hell... he'd probably burned it or otherwise destroyed it just to get rid of the written evidence of the type of monster he was.

She stood there and peered into the townhouse, watching her father. He sat still in the recliner, moving only to sip from a can of beer that was resting in the fork of his legs. He did not look antsy or anxious in any way. The act of breaking, entering, and petty theft apparently did not bother him all that much.

She wasn't sure how long she stood there. It was mesmerizing to watch this figure from her past, now frozen in the present with no clear direction or purpose. It was hard to look away from him. Seeing him in such a natural way made him look nothing like a monster, but instead like a miserable old man who had nothing left to live for.

She would likely have stood there much longer, trying to process it all if she could.

But then her phone rang in her pocket.

The noise of it alarmed her so badly that she took a huge lumbering step away from the door. She reached into her pocket to silence it and as she did, she just barely caught sight of her father sitting up in his chair and looking to the back door. She was quite certain he had not seen her, but he was getting up, clearly having heard the strange noise on his back porch.

"Shit," Chloe breathed as she leaped down the small flight of stairs. She then bolted to the right, in the direction of the darkened corner and the shrouded recycle bins. Just as she reached the corner, sprinting as hard yet as quietly as she could, she heard the muffled sound of a door opening.

She slid around the corner and waited. She focused as hard as she could, listening for the sound of footsteps. When she heard nothing, she chanced a glance around the edge of the building. Her father was there, his back to her as he slightly leaned over the porch railing to investigate.

Not wanting to tempt fate any farther, Chloe slowly walked back toward the parking lot. She passed the recycle bins and the air conditioning units, stepping back into the glow of the streetlights in the parking lot. She got into her car and sat still for a moment, looking toward the townhouse. A million thoughts rolled through her mind as she tried to think of the best course of action to take from here.

She took out her phone and looked to see who had called while she had been snooping. She wasn't surprised to see that it had been Rhodes. She nearly called her back but before she did so, one last thought occurred to her. It might be risky and a bit unprofessional, but it made a great deal of sense in that moment.

She placed a call to the local PD, using the same number that had come across her display earlier in the day when Officer Henley had called to tell her that someone had broken into her apartment. When the phone was answered on the other end, it was not Henley but a receptionist. When she asked for Henley, she was placed on hold and then transferred to Henley's cell phone.

"This is Henley," the officer said on the other end.

"Officer Henley, this is Agent Fine. You told me to call if you could be of any further help."

"Of course," Henley said, sounding surprised. "What do you need?"

"Well, first of all, I need to ask that what I am about to ask of you stays between us. I don't expect you to break any rules or go against any of your captain's orders, but if you could keep it quiet and just between us, that would be best."

"Um...well, I'd like to, but that sounds suspicious. I really don't feel like getting involved in anything that's going to piss my captain off."

"No, it's nothing like that. Look...I have a suspicion about who it might have been that broke into my place. But I don't have nearly enough evidence or enough probable cause to take it to my section director. I just need you to sort of keep an eye on someone. Drive by every now and then, keep an ear out for anything that comes over the wires, that sort of thing."

"Oh. Well, yeah, I guess I could do that. What's the name?"

"Aiden Fine." She also gave Henley the address.

"Got it. Is it a relative or something?"

"Yeah...or something."

"I'll do my best to keep tabs on him. You doing good since the break-in? Did the guys ever come by to dust for prints?"

"Yeah. Thanks again for your help."

Chloe ended the call and once again looked back to her father's place. Without taking her eyes away from it, she placed a call to Rhodes. Rhodes answered right away, sounding a little tired and frustrated.

"Hey, Fine. Everything good? You left in a hurry."

"Yeah. Just...some strained personal stuff."

There was a tense silence where Chloe could all but hear Rhodes thinking—trying to decide if she should ask what sort of stuff or just keep it professional. In the end, she decided on professionalism.

"Well, I just wanted to give you an update. Rachel Dobbs left the station about an hour and a half ago. I wrapped up a bit of paperwork with Deputy Nolan and am currently headed home."

"What did you learn about that woman Rachel mentioned right before I left?"

"Gwen Ingram. And I learned plenty...enough to know for a fact that we'll be visiting her first thing tomorrow."

It was refreshing to know that they at least had a solid place to start the case tomorrow. But as she sat there in front of her father's townhouse, Chloe wasn't too sure she'd be able to give the case her full attention.

It made her all the more certain that her life would never truly be fully her own until she brought this sordid chapter with her father to a close.

CHAPTER FOURTEEN

Danielle was hungry but could not eat. Her stomach was in knots. Her nerves were fried. She'd attempted to eat microwaved chicken nuggets but had stopped at two. The rest of them sat on a plate on her coffee table directly beside the item that was causing her severe anxiety.

Her mother's diary.

Honestly, it wasn't the diary itself that had her feeling somewhat sick. It was what she had done earlier in the day to get the diary. She had nearly changed her mind twice on the way over to Chloe's place. She had done some seedy and deplorable things in the past, but nothing quite this deliberate. She hated the idea that she had, for all intents and purposes, stolen from Chloe.

More than that, she had left her apartment a mess. But that had been part of it. She wanted it to seem like whoever had been there had been in a hurry. She figured leaving a mess would make it seem more urgent…more like their father.

Another reason Danielle was unable to eat much of anything was because of the notes she had found in the back of the diary. They were written on a plain piece of printer paper, folded neatly and tucked between the last page and the back cover. The paper was filled with Chloe's thin, small handwriting.

It seemed that Chloe had been doing some freelance detective work for herself, going through the diary and putting some of the pieces together. And based on what she had uncovered so far, Danielle didn't blame her for being quiet and reserved when she had paid a visit the other day.

Chloe had gone through and found entries in the diary and then done her best to align them with times from their childhood where their mother had been sick or out of sorts. There were two listings on Chloe's little note sheet that seemed to reach out and smack Danielle directly in the face.

Entry, p.11: Mom says dad hit her in the head with a beer bottle when she told him he needed to stop drinking. It was summer...just before me and D went back to school. This lines up with mom telling us that she had fallen down the front porch stoop when trying to bring in groceries. RE; the bruising over her eyes for a few weeks.

Entry, p. 35: Mom says dad got rough with her in bed. Slapped her around, got really violent. She asked him to stop and he punched her in the stomach. Essentially raped her. Vaginally and anally. She bled most of the night. This lines up with the day D discovered bloody sheets when doing laundry. When she asked, Dad told her to shut up and do her chores like a good girl (I remember this!). It was also during that time that mom said she had severe migraines and stayed in her room with the blinds drawn for a few days.

There were several other notes jotted down in Chloe's handwriting, but those two were the most powerful. Danielle figured in a court of law, it would be more than enough to cast a suspicious eye on their father. Even as she looked over the notes, Danielle could remember both of those instances—her mother wearing sunglasses when she dropped her and Chloe off for their first day of third grade (or had it been fourth?); the sheets with bloody splotch marks on them that her father got enraged over for some reason while their mother was holed up like a prisoner in the bedroom.

She remembered all of it. And now, apparently, so did Chloe. And Chloe was making connections now...seeing the real face of their father.

So why was she not doing anything about it yet?

At the bottom of Chloe's notes there was a small box with another alarming set of information. It was titled **Threats of Violence or Death.** Chloe had given page numbers of each instance. There were eight in all.

Danielle noticed that Chloe had not marked her mother's diary up in any way, though. She apparently did not want to taint it—whether for sentiment's sake or for some future lawful use, Danielle could not be sure.

The longer Danielle stared at Chloe's notes, the more another feeling started to settle in around her heart. She could not name it at first but as she thought about the last year and everything that had to happen to get Chloe to see her father for what he truly was, the feelings became easier to identify.

Betrayal.

There was enough evidence in the journal itself as well as within Chloe's notes to nail the bastard again. Of course, she knew the slightest bit about the law and wondered if this would fall under double jeopardy—the term that stated a person could not be convicted of the same exact crime twice.

She didn't know the ins and outs of all of it. But Chloe probably did … and she was choosing to do absolutely nothing about it.

The hell of it was that Danielle couldn't call the police anyway. After all, it had been *her* that had broken into Chloe's apartment to steal the book. She'd worn gloves and, just to be safe, had taped up the bottoms of her shoes. She was fairly certain she would never be discovered, so going to the police with the diary and having to explain how she had come across it would certainly cause problems.

She wanted to storm out right then and there to confront her sister. But she was too angry and that would only lead to a very messy confrontation … and anyway, she wasn't quite ready to admit to breaking in. She'd much prefer to take that little secret to the grave with her.

And if she could find some way to get around it, that was exactly what she would do.

She picked the diary back up again and started to read, wondering if there was something Chloe had found that she had missed—something that would make her sister sit on such damning evidence rather than using it to finally do away with their father.

CHAPTER FIFTEEN

When Chloe rolled out of bed the following day, the first thing she did was finish cleaning up. Her father had left one hell of a mess and the longer she left it all scattered around the apartment, the longer she'd have to face the fact of what he had done. She spent a few minutes cleaning, taking in the morning's first cup of coffee as she sorted out her thoughts.

As she cleaned, she did her best to switch her mindset. She had to push her father and the diary to the back of her mind and focus solely on the Jessie Fairchild case. It was easier to do when Rhodes called to let her know she was heading back to Falls Church, having to return the loaner car she'd had to borrow from the PD after Chloe had left suddenly.

Chloe tidied up a few more things and then headed for the door shortly after 7:30. She looked back into the mostly cleaned apartment and tried to imagine her father rummaging through it all. More than that, she tried to think of what he might look like raising up his leg and kicking her door down.

For the slightest of moments, she could not see it. Age and prison had not been kind to him. It would take a lot of force for him to knock the door in hard enough to break it free from the chain lock.

But she could not let that occupy her mind … not right now.

She headed out of the apartment, doing everything she could to slip back into the role of talented field agent and out of the role of dejected daughter.

❧   ❧   ❧

After meeting back up at the Falls Church Police Department, Chloe and Rhodes wasted no time in heading out to the residence of Gwen and Bill Ingram. It was, unsurprisingly, located in the same high-scale subdivision the Fairchilds lived in. The Ingram house was tucked away in a cul-de-sac on the other side of the subdivision from the Fairchild house. It was, in Chloe's estimation, the nicest house in the neighborhood—and that was saying something.

They'd called ahead to ensure Gwen would be there to speak with them, but there was a very long pause after Rhodes knocked on the door. Chloe found herself almost wishing for the warm (albeit fake) response she had received from Candace Derringer yesterday, with her fresh coffee and bagels.

When the door *was* answered, it was by a tired and disheveled woman. With some makeup, she might look like all of the other housewives in the neighborhood, but Gwen Ingram currently looked like she had gone several rounds with sleepless nights and depression. The only thing made up about her was her hair. It looked like it had been recently colored and styled. The shade of red in her hair was almost unnatural but was also quite striking on her.

Despite her somewhat haggard appearance, Gwen managed a thin smile as she regarded Chloe and Rhodes.

"Mrs. Ingram?" Chloe asked.

"Yeah, that's me. You the agents?"

"Yes, ma'am," Chloe said, showing her badge. "Agents Fine and Rhodes. Can we come in?"

"Yes, please…"

Gwen led them through a large foyer with high ceilings. She did not engage them at all, simply walking forward with hunched shoulders as she led them into what Chloe assumed served as some sort of parlor or sitting room. Gwen sat down in a beautiful ornate chair, leaving Chloe and Rhodes to sit in a large plush sofa against the far wall.

"You wanted to talk about Jessie Fairchild, right?" Gwen asked.

"That's correct," Chloe said. "Would that be okay with you?"

"Oh, I don't care. But honestly, there's not much to tell. I made an ass out of myself one Saturday afternoon right there on the street outside of my house and it was all because of her."

Rhodes nodded. "We have someone within the neighborhood that told me about the altercation. But do you think you could tell us about it in your own words?"

Gwen shrugged, as if it really wasn't a big deal at all. "Look... I'm sort of the gossip of the neighborhood... probably this entire corner of town, really. Did your *source* tell you about all the trouble my husband has been in?"

"No," Rhodes said. "They were very respectful of your privacy."

"Hmm. Then why are you here at all?" Gwen then let out a sigh and relaxed against the back of the chair. "Bill was always a good husband. He worked hard but not hard enough so that we never saw one another. It's not a secret that he was making very good money as the leading attorney with the biggest law firm in the city—the fifth biggest in the state. But Bill has always had something of a troubled side... I think it came from the way he was raised, honestly. But he's always had a drinking problem. Not bad enough that I ever gave him a hard time about it, but bad enough to make me worry. Not until last year, that is. Something happened to him—I don't know what... probably something at work that he never told me about—and the drinking got worse. I'd watch him fill his flask with bourbon in the morning, putting it in his briefcase and heading out to work like it was nothing."

"I'm sorry to interrupt," Chloe said, "but does your husband have anything to do with Jessie Fairchild?"

"In a roundabout way. Now, would you please let me finish this?"

Chloe nodded respectfully and said nothing else.

"Bill had been working on this major case for a nuclear decommissioning agency for about two years and he was *this close* to bringing it to the finish line. Over the last three months or so, he started to tell me that this could be big for him—for *us*. He was set to make nearly eleven million dollars off of his end of it and that the win would change the face of the firm. But then he botched one meeting. And then another and another. I still don't know all of the details, but they lost the case. Bill drove off the day after they lost and ran his car into the back of a bus. He was fine but the cops on the scene saw that he was drunk. Apparently, his bosses knew he had been drinking but let it slide. But then, after botching the case so badly and losing it for them—as well as the reckless driving—they fired him.

"That was two months ago. Ever since then, Bill comes and goes as he pleases. His family has a cabin up at Niagara Falls and his sister keeps calling me to tell me that's where he's at. He's drinking himself stupid, but quite frankly, I don't care. Let him get it out of his system. He loves me … he'll come back home to me. But we would have to leave this neighborhood. We have a lot of money saved up, but living here, we'd go through it quicker than we'd like.

"Anyway … where Jessie Fairchild comes into play is that she somehow heard this entire story. It got around the neighborhood quickly, as stories like that tend to. I had spoken to Jessie a few times. She seemed nice enough … maybe a little snobby. But not the sort of stuck up snobby you'd expect; I don't think she even knew she was coming off that way. But she came over two weeks ago. Said she had heard about what happened and told me that her father had a drinking problem that he eventually overcame. That pissed me off, her thinking she could relate or sympathize, but I kept quiet. But then she said she would be willing to lend me some money if Bill was making things hard. And … well, I lost it. I snapped."

"How so?" Chloe asked.

"Well, we were on the porch drinking tea when we had the talk. And when I snapped, I tossed the entire table over and asked her to leave. To her credit, she walked down the stairs and did as I asked, but I kept going. All of the pent up frustration and anger I had felt over Bill and the drinking and the situation at his work … I let it out on her. And honestly … I wish I could tell you I felt bad about it, but I didn't."

"How bad did it get?" Rhodes asked.

"I chased her down the steps, screaming at her. Called her a bitch and a...well, another word I never thought I'd use and won't repeat here or ever again—it begins with a C. I raised my hand back to slap her but thank God I somehow restrained myself."

"And why all the hate for her? Did you feel some beforehand?"

"A little. I'd seen how she'd all but unseated Rachel Dobbs from her little socialite perch at the silent auction. If I'm being real with you....it's just because she was new. Here she was, this beautiful and wealthy woman, new to the neighborhood and basically forcing herself into the social circles. And meanwhile, I'm essentially on my way out...with my alcoholic husband."

"Mrs. Ingram...if you don't mind my asking, where were you last Friday morning between eight and noon?"

"I had a hair appointment at nine," she said, tugging at her red hair. "Got a color, a cut, the whole nine yards. For most women, shopping or vegging out cheers them up. For me, it's getting my hair done."

Chloe again looked at her hair. It did look very pretty, though a bit in-your-face. It made her wonder what her natural hair color was.

"How long were you there?" Rhodes asked.

"I don't know. The whole process took about an hour and a half. But after that, I went out and had lunch with a friend of mine. I know where you're trying to go with this...and I can give you the names and number of people that I interacted with that morning."

"I don't think that will be necessary just now," Chloe said. "I do appreciate your honesty, and I think we'll get out of your hair for now."

Gwen smiled, not sure if the *out of your hair* comment was a joke or not. "Let me show you out, then," she said.

Chloe and Rhodes followed after her, Chloe walking a little closer than was necessary. When they got to the door, Gwen followed them out onto the porch.

"I was very sorry to hear what happened to her," Gwen said. "While I was infuriated that she had offered to loan me some money—even though I barely knew her—I had no doubt she would have done it. Rich and oblivious or not, I think she was a good soul when you got right down to it."

Chloe stepped out of her comfort zone and reached out. She placed a reassuring hand on Gwen's shoulder and said, "Again, thanks for sharing all of that. It couldn't be easy."

"It is what it is."

"Let us know if you can think of anything else that might help with our investigation," Chloe said as she and Rhodes walked down the stairs to their car.

Inside the car, as she cranked it to life, Rhodes looked over at Chloe with a weird smile. "Okay...what did you find?"

Chloe showed Rhodes her right hand...the same hand she'd used to reassure Gwen with. It currently held two distinct hairs.

"Are those Gwen's?" Rhodes asked.

"They were on the shoulder of her shirt."

Rhodes leaned closer and squinted at them. "Looks red to me."

"Look here, though," Chloe said, pinching the hair near the end—near the root.

"Blonde," Rhodes said.

"And the stray hair found at the Fairchild residence was..."

"Blonde," Rhodes finished.

"Not a smoking gun by any means," Chloe said. "But given that Gwen's hair had been so recently colored, it's worth looking into. I think we should get this hair to forensics."

"Sounds like a plan," Rhodes said as she pulled back out into the street.

Chloe looked into the rearview and was a little unnerved to see that Gwen Ingram was standing at the top of her stairs, watching them leave.

Chapter Sixteen

Chloe's phone rang on the way back to the station. She answered it and discovered Nolan on the other end.

"Agent Fine, where are you at the moment?"

"Leaving Gwen Ingram's house. Why? What do you need?"

"Well, the sister is on the way here…Jessie's sister, Bev Givens."

"Great. Any idea why it took so long for her to respond to calls?"

"Yeah. Apparently, she went camping with her family somewhere in Gloucester. Cut their phones off and everything, just her, her daughter, and her husband. So she just now got a shitload of messages about what happened."

"Oh my God. Has she spoken with Mark yet?"

"Yes. Mark is planning to meet with them later today."

"But the sister—Bev—she's on the way to the station?"

"She is. Maybe twenty minutes out at this point. I don't think they even went home; they're coming straight here from the campsite."

"We're on the way. And hey, go ahead and make a call to forensics. We have some hair samples for them."

"Will do."

"Who is Bev?" Rhodes asked when Chloe ended the call.

"Bev Givens…Jessie Fairchild's sister. Apparently, she had been camping with her family and their cell phones were turned off."

"Sounds miserable."

"The camping or coming back home to such terrible news?"

Rhodes smirked a little and said: "Can I say both?"

❧   ❧   ❧

When they got back to the station, Nolan was waiting for them with an evidence bag for the hair. He was quick and efficient, bagging it up and already having filled out the necessary forms for forensics when they came by. He did this all while also directing them to the back of the building where Bev Givens had been taken less than a minute ago.

Nolan left the bag for forensics with the station receptionist and followed Chloe and Rhodes to the back of the building. Bev had been taken to the same room they had used to speak with Mark Fairchild, as if they were trying to keep the mystery and sorrow away from the rest of the station.

"Before we go in, you should know something," Nolan said. "She clearly hasn't truly processed it yet. She's trying to remain logical, trying to help find answers. But you can see her breaking. She could snap at any moment…and I don't think it's going to be pretty."

With a solemn look, Nolan opened the door to the little conference room and ushered the agents in. Chloe saw a thin middle-aged woman sitting at a table. She looked very much like Jessie Fairchild. Bev was a bit leaner and slightly taller. Her hair was a lighter shade of brown but other than that, Bev and Jessie could have easily passed for twins back in their younger days.

A man sat beside her, his arm protectively around her. He regarded Chloe and Rhodes with the sort of hope that usually broke Chloe's heart a little. This, Chloe assumed, was Bev's husband.

"Mrs. Givens, we're Agents Fine and Rhodes," Chloe said. "Thanks for coming in to speak with us so quickly."

"Of course. I understand there aren't really many answers to be had. I want to help however I can."

"I'm her husband," the man next to her confirmed. "Roger Givens. I'm also eager to help any way I can. But I'd prefer to stay by Bev's side."

"That's perfectly fine," Chloe said. "And Mrs. Givens, you're right. We don't have many answers and each day that passes makes the case a little harder to solve. So please keep that in mind if these questions seem quick or even harsh."

She nodded her understanding and when she did, Chloe saw what Nolan had mentioned. There was a vacantness to her stare. It was like watching someone stare contemplatively out of a rainy window, thinking deep about something that troubled them. But it was only in her eyes; the rest of her expression seemed a little unsure of how she should be reacting.

"We understand you were camping when this happened," Chloe said. "When did you leave to start the trip?"

"We left home Friday morning," Bev said. "Got to the campground around noon, I guess."

"And your phones were off the entire time?"

"Yes. It was a way for us to reconnect as a family. Our daughter spends way too much time on her phone, so we designed this whole screen-free weekend. And I'm pretty sure she hated every minute of it."

"Where is your daughter now?" Rhodes asked.

"With Mark. He…oh my God…he tried calling me. No one knew where we were…just the people we worked for. Is that terrible?"

"There's no way you could have known this would happen," Rhodes assured her.

"So, I assume you stayed until this morning, correct?" Chloe asked.

"That's right. Woke up, had breakfast, and tore everything down."

"We didn't even think to turn our phones on until we got on the road," Roger Givens said. "And when we did … we saw everything we had missed."

"Mark told me most of the details," Bev said. "And I just still can't believe it."

"Mrs. Givens, do either of you know if there were circumstances other than Mark's job that caused them to move away from Boston?"

"Just the job," Bev said. "I think Jessie was looking forward to the move. She was never really a big-city kind of girl."

"They weren't here for very long... did you ever speak to her while she was living here?"

"A few times. Three, maybe. On the phone. Jessie and I... we weren't very close. No bad blood or anything. Just... we drifted apart after she left for college and we never truly reconnected. She married Mark and that became her life. Lots of money and vacations and just this whole other life I couldn't even begin to imagine."

"Would you say she flaunted her wealth?" Rhodes asked.

"God no," she said with a sad little smile. "If anything, I think she was very uneasy with it. Even up until the moment they moved here, I don't think she ever really got used to it. I think it's one of the reasons she was always trying to do some good with it."

"What do you mean?" Chloe asked. "What sort of *good*?"

"Oh, it was so much. She and Mark would give so much to different organizations and fundraisers. Fundraisers for cancer, donations to things like the Humane Society, local reading programs, Special Olympics, things like that. A few years back, I'm pretty sure she gave just about every cent she made in one calendar year to some sort of fund in Boston to help pay for medical bills for those affected by the marathon bombing. Of course, she could do that sort of thing because Mark is loaded."

"Please forgive me for asking this," Chloe said, "but I have to make sure I have a clear picture here. This was all charitable giving, it sounds like. Was she that sort of person or do you think they, as a couple, used it as posturing?"

"No. Mark wasn't like that, either. They were both very kind people... a match made in heaven, really. Sometime a few years ago, they took a trip to Puerto Rico, right after those terrible hurricanes. They told no one where they were going or what they were doing. I only know this because I sort of tricked her into telling me. But they went down there and checked out some of the rebuilding efforts. Donated a ton of money to the cause. They were there for about a week and I think they *maybe* used a day to themselves, doing beach stuff... tourist stuff."

Chloe slowly mulled all of this over. Sure, the source of information might be somewhat biased, but it was also easily applicable to what she had gathered about Jessie's time in Falls Church. Maybe she wasn't trying to join all of those organizations just to fit in or find ways to flaunt her status. Maybe she was legitimately wanting to help—and the majority of the other wealthy women in town weren't able to see it yet.

"Back in Boston … do you know of anyone who may have held a grudge against your sister?"

Bev looked to Roger and they chuckled nervously. They shook their heads in unison. "No, not at all," Bev said.

"Everyone loved her and Mark," Roger said. "And I'm not just saying that to make them seem like super nice people. It's the truth. I can give you any number of names to go speak with and you'll hear the same thing."

"I think maybe I should say this, though," Bev said. "Not the last time I spoke to Jessie, but the time before that, she talked about how she was afraid Mark might be overworking himself after the move. She said he was sort of distant and depressed … and those were two things she had never seen out of him."

"Did she give any particular reasons why she felt that way?"

"No. She just said she was worried about him. She thought maybe the move and the new location was trickier than he had thought. But it didn't seem like anything serious … just something Jessie mentioned almost in a passing sort of way."

"But she didn't go into any more detail than that?" Rhodes asked.

"No. She wasn't the type to speak ill about her husband … even when it came down to things he might be struggling with."

As Chloe lined up her next question, she felt her phone vibrate in her pocket. She checked in quickly, not wanting to be rude to a sibling who had just lost her sister. She did not recognize the number that was calling so she passed it off and concentrated on her next question.

"Do you know if there were ever any marital problems between them, no matter how small?"

"Again … if they did, I didn't know about it. They were always so happy. They were always…"

There was a flicker that briefly crossed Bev's face as the sadness of the situation—and potentially the reality of it all—seemed to catch up with her.

"Can we be done now?" she asked. "I'm happy to help but right now … can I just…"

"You're fine," Chloe said. "Please, yes, go. And take your time."

Bev nodded, though she looked sad that she had not been able to offer more information. "Thank you…"

Roger also gave a quick nod of thanks and appreciation as the couple made their way out of the room.

"What do you think?" Rhodes asked when the door was closed behind the couple.

"I think my initial reaction may not be professional. But I'll say it anyway. If these donations Bev is talking about were really made, there would be tax information and likely even receipts to back it up. Same with the Puerto Rico trip. And if it all pans out, I'd be inclined to think that all of the women we spoke to so far are nothing but jealous bitches. And that makes me angry."

"I'm there right along with you," Rhodes said.

Letting it stew and simmer for a moment, Chloe took out her phone. She checked the display and saw that the unknown number that had called had not left a message.

"Someone called while we were speaking with her," Chloe told Rhodes as she pressed the number and placed a return call. "Maybe one of the jealous bitches."

She meant it to sound lighthearted but it came out with some barb. The phone rang twice on the other end before it was picked up by a woman with a cheery voice.

"Hello?"

"This is Agent Chloe Fine. Someone called me from this number."

"Yes, Agent Fine…this is Candace Derringer. You told me to give you a call if I heard anything that might help with the case. And I think I might have something."

"What is it?" Chloe asked, recalling the almost nonchalant way Candace Derringer had discussed Jessie Fairchild over bagels and coffee on her porch.

"Well, I'm sure it's no surprise to you that the presence of the FBI has made its way around the gossip circles. I've had a few ladies on my porch this morning talking about it."

"You mean gossiping about it." Chloe couldn't help it; the comment came out before she could bite it back.

"Sadly, yes. But there is some good to come from it. I've heard from two very reliable sources that maybe Jessie Fairchild *did* make something of an enemy not too long before she was killed."

"Who would that be?"

"A woman named Evelyn Marshall. I've heard the story twice and it was quite different both times…so maybe you should hear it directly from her."

"I'd love to," Chloe said. "Do you have her number?"

"Of course," Candace said with a proud little laugh. "Agent, I have *everyone's* number."

Chloe bit down the smart remark that sprang to her tongue as she wrote the number down, hoping for a promising lead.

CHAPTER SEVENTEEN

Immediately after telling Deputy Nolan where they were going, Chloe and Rhodes left the station yet again. It was getting later in the afternoon and the day was starting to feel quite long ... which was disheartening, given that they hadn't really discovered all that much. They arrived at the Marshall residence at 4:35. A single car was parked in the U-shaped driveway, dwarfed by the massive size of the house.

It was located on a strip of land that looked to be at least twenty acres, the backyard a massive sprawling sheet of green, broken by rosebushes and a pool that was connected to the house by a spacious back deck. It was not located in a neighborhood, but about four miles away from any sort of neighborhood at all. It was isolated from everything, as if it was too good to be in the presence of other homes.

"I'd love to say this place looks pretentious," Rhodes said. "But ... damn, this is a beautiful house."

Chloe agreed, but said nothing. As they got out of the car, she noted that the car in the driveway did not really seem to fit in alongside the house. It was an older model Honda Accord, no more recent than a 2005 model. *Maybe they're so rich because they skimp on certain areas,* she thought.

They walked up the stairs, the porch ceiling towering at least ten feet over their heads. Chloe rang the doorbell; it sounded like ancient church bells on the other side of the house—a house she didn't doubt was nearly hollowed out in its enormity.

It took a while for the door to be answered. The woman who opened the door was not at all what Chloe had been expecting. It was a younger woman—maybe thirty at most—who looked rather mousy. "Can I help you?" she asked.

"Yes, we're Agents Fine and Rhodes, with the FBI," Chloe said. "We're looking for Evelyn Marshall."

"Well, you've got the right house. But you just missed her by about twenty minutes."

"Where did she go?" Rhodes asked.

"She and her husband are headed to the airport. They're taking a trip to St. Croix for two weeks."

Well, that certainly seems convenient, Chloe thought. But before jumping to any conclusions, she knew she had to get a better idea of who Evelyn Marshall truly was.

"And who are you, exactly?" Chloe asked.

"I'm Emma Ramsey, the Marshalls' nanny. They hired me to watch Declan—their two-year-old—and house sit while they're gone."

"And how long have you worked for them?"

"Since Declan was about six months old. So a year and a half, I guess."

"Do you mind answering a few questions for us?"

Emma looked back into the house awkwardly and then back to the agents. "I'd invite you in, but they are really strict about strangers being in their house. But Declan is down for his afternoon nap, so if you want, we can just hang out here, on the porch. He'll wake up any minute now, though … I was afraid the doorbell would do it, but he's still snoozing."

"Here on the porch is just fine," Chloe said.

"FBI … is there something wrong?" There was something in Emma's tone that made Chloe think maybe Emma *wanted* something to be wrong.

"Well, we're looking into a specific crime here in town and Evelyn's name was given to us as someone who might know a thing or two about it. Or, at the very least, to be able to direct us to people who might know a great deal more than she does."

It wasn't a total lie, so Chloe didn't feel too bad about misleading her a bit.

"What crime?" Emma asked.

"I can't say just yet. But we just need you to give us your honest appraisal of Evelyn. And we need you to be as transparent and honest as possible. Nothing you say to us will be passed on to her. We need total honesty here."

"How honest?"

"Very. And it goes no farther than the three of us, right here in this moment."

"I can do that. The woman is a raging bitch most of the time. If I'm being honest." She looked like admitting it released a massive weight from her shoulders. "But not in a loud and obnoxious or obvious way. It's a quiet brooding...the sort of bitch that doesn't make you hate her necessarily, but makes you hate yourself. You know what I mean?"

"I think I do. But can you explain a bit more?"

"Well, she likes to control people. Like, if she catches a friend in a lie or something like that, she seems all forgiving at first. But then she has no problem weaponizing that lie and threatening to use it against them in the future. I don't know for sure, but I feel like she's probably been doing that for quite a while. There's a rumor going around town that she has some huge dirt on her husband and that's the only reason he hasn't left her. Something about an affair. I don't know that there's any truth to it, though."

"Has she ever been emotionally or physically abusive to you in any way?"

"Oh, she'll yell at me all of the time. For small things. But she never does it in front of company. Hell, she never even does it in front of Declan."

"Does she have a reputation for showing off her money?" Rhodes asked.

"It depends on what you mean by showing off. She's from a very rich family—one of those families that made a fortune farming tobacco in the seventies and eighties. That's where the bulk of her money comes from; when her parents died, they left her everything. But she's made some business deals on the side, selling some of the family farmland to environmental groups that want to use it for solar and wind power. She's a very rich woman...and her husband is almost as rich as she is. So, no...she doesn't flaunt her wealth. She doesn't have to. People just know."

"Do you know a woman named Jessie Fairchild?" Chloe asked.

Emma thought about it for a moment, a stern look on her face. "I don't think so," she said. "But the name *does* sound familiar."

"What about any recent altercations Evelyn might have had with someone?"

"Oh, for sure," Emma said, actually stifling back a bit of a laugh. "That was as recent as last Tuesday night. Evelyn tried to keep it quiet, but you know how the gossip circles in these kinds of towns can be."

"Do you have any details?"

"Yes, I do. And I haven't shared it because it just adds fuel to the fire. But I gathered all of what happened because I was over here the following morning. Between hearing her and her husband talk about it, and conversations she had on the phone, I gathered just about the entire story. See, there's this fundraiser Evelyn puts on every year—she organizes it and pays for just about everything. It's for local emergency services and it's this whole gala type thing. And even though it's to raise money for emergency services, Evelyn is the Queen Bee of it all. It puts her right there in the spotlight. But apparently, someone else showed up and sort of took that spotlight off of her last week. Evelyn was pissed."

Must be nice for something so petty to be considered a problem, Chloe thought, ruminating on her own personal problems.

"Do you have a name for this person?" she asked.

"No. I just kept hearing Evelyn refer to her as new. Some woman that was new to the area."

"You said the name Jessie Fairchild sounded familiar to you," Rhodes said. "Do you think she could have been the new woman?"

"It could have been, sure. But I'd just be speculating, honestly."

"Do you have any details about what happened?" Chloe asked.

"Well, from what I gather, this woman was meeting with higher-ups at this event and promising to make donations. Evelyn caught wind of it and pulled her to the side. Why, I don't know. Maybe to tell her it was her show and she was butting in and stealing her lime-light. Apparently, the conversation escalated into this huge thing. Evelyn even told one of her friends on the phone that she should have shut up when she realized people were looking at her. She said this new woman was even on her way out, trying to avoid making a scene but Evelyn kept going. She was bad about that—not knowing to shut up when she really got going. But this woman stopped at the door as she was leaving and must have said something...I don't know what. What I do know is that part of what she said included her calling Evelyn *petty* and *small-time*. And those are two words no one has ever called Evelyn Marshall."

"You're certain all of this is factual?" Chloe asked.

"I heard it all directly from Evelyn's mouth."

Behind Emma, from the small crack she had left in the door, they could all hear the gentle fussing of a toddler walking up from a nap. A small, delicate voice called out: "Em? Where you?"

"That's me," Emma said, turning to head inside.

"Thanks for your time," Chloe said. "Quickly, before you go back inside...do you happen to know the flight information for this trip to St. Croix?"

"Sorry...no."

"Make and model of the car they were driving?"

"A 2019 Escalade. White."

"We can work with that. Thanks again. Oh! One more question..."

"Yeah?" Emma asked, clearly torn between spilling details on Evelyn and her duties as a responsible nanny.

"What color is Evelyn's hair?"

"She's a blonde...though it's starting to go gray."

"Thanks."

Emma nodded and headed back inside, closing the door behind her. Chloe and Rhodes hurried down the steps to the car.

"We rushing to the airport, I take it?" Rhodes asked.

"We are," Chloe said, getting behind the wheel. "Get Nolan on the phone. Give him the description of the car and see if he can get us a plate number. I want to talk to Evelyn Marshall before she has the chance to skip town."

"It *does* seem convenient, huh? The timing of the trip, I mean."

"It absolutely does."

Rhodes called up Nolan as she had been asked as Chloe sped down the road, headed for the interstate and Ronald Reagan Washington National Airport beyond.

CHAPTER EIGHTEEN

The drive to the airport was a quick one, as only twenty-eight miles separated Evelyn Marshall's home from the airport entrance. Along the way, Rhodes made a few calls, first to Nolan and then to airport security, instructing them to attempt to locate and potentially detain a passenger that could be arriving any minute, by the name of Evelyn Marshall.

As Rhodes was on the phone taking care of all of this, Chloe received a call. She did not recognize the number but when on a case like this, where things suddenly seemed to be moving along quite fast, that did not matter. She answered it as she maintained a speed of eighty-five on the interstate.

"This is Agent Fine," she answered.

"Agent Fine, this is Deanna Riotti with the Northern Virginia Forensics Lab. I've got some preliminary results for you on a hair sample that was rushed to us by Deputy Nolan out in Falls Church."

"Great. What do you have for me?"

"This hair sample taken from one Rachel Dobbs does not appear to be a match to the sample taken from the crime scene of Jessica Fairchild's murder. Let me stress ... these are just preliminary findings. Nolan indicated you needed results quickly, so I wanted to give you *something*."

"Thanks," Chloe said. "Just so I'm clear ... there are still tests than need to be run, but based on initial findings, there's no match?"

"Correct. And about ninety percent of the time, these preliminary findings turn out to be the end result as well."

"Thanks for the update," Chloe said, ending the call and returning her full attention to road ahead.

Rhodes, having just ended a call herself, looked over to her with anticipation and a bit of excitement in her eyes. "Forensics?"

"Yeah. The hair I got from Dobbs isn't a match to the one found at the crime scene."

"Which makes Evelyn Marshall even more interesting," Rhodes commented.

Chloe nodded her agreement and pressed down a little harder on the gas.

They arrived at the airport eleven minutes later, with a police escort waiting at the primary entrance. Chloe followed the flashing lights ahead of them, following them to a roundabout side entrance. There seemed to be an afternoon rush of traffic along the entrance, so the escort saved them a great deal of time.

Chloe parked directly beside the patrol car at a small lot tucked away between the multiple gates and employee entrances not too far away from the central baggage area. The place was an absolute madhouse of motion as they joined the police officer who had served as their escort.

"Thanks for the assist," Chloe said as they followed him to a side door.

"Sure thing. I got word on the way in that an air marshal detained your suspect. She did not go lightly, though. They nabbed her just as she was checking her bags. She's currently in one of our holding rooms."

They entered the airport through a small employee lounge. The escort led them through the room, through two additional doors, and then into the airport. After cutting directly across the concourse, he then led them behind one of the security check-ins and down a hall marked *Authorized Personnel Only*.

Having never been involved in a case that was in any way attached to an airport, this was all new to Chloe. She felt like she was treading on sacred ground, getting a peek at one of the busier buildings within the DC metro area.

The hallway ended in a T-intersection. The wall in front of them contained five rooms, all marked with letters A through E. To the right, closer to the A door, came a shrill voice, booming and obnoxious. It was an enraged female ... surely Evelyn Marshall. Sure enough, that was exactly where the escort led them.

He knocked on the door, waited a beat, and then entered. The blaring noise of the female voice was louder now, unobstructed by the door. They entered as Evelyn Marshall finished up a statement ending with something about her "basic human rights."

There were four uniformed officers in the room, Two appeared to be policemen, while the others were either air marshals or airport security. Chloe saw that they had cuffed Evelyn. It made her frown, as it seemed a bit much. If Evelyn decided to make a fuss about this entire thing, she could potentially use that against them.

"These are the agents," the escort told the four officers in the room.

"Agents Rhodes and Fine," Rhodes said.

"She's cuffed," Chloe pointed out. "Was that really necessary?"

"It was," one of the non-policemen said. She was pretty sure he was indeed a member of airport security. "She basically went crazy when we asked her to step away from the baggage desk. In her outburst, her flailing elbow struck a thirteen-year-old girl standing behind her. So yes ... she's cuffed."

Chloe nodded her understanding. "Can we please have the room?"

The four authority figures nodded almost in unison. It appeared that they were more than happy to be out of Evelyn Marshall's presence. The escort dipped out right along with them, closing the door behind him. This left Chloe and Rhodes alone with Evelyn. She looked much younger than Chloe had been expecting. But she also looked like a caged animal—ready to tear a throat out at any given moment, but frightened as well. She tossed some of her long blonde hair over her shoulder and regarded Chloe and Rhodes as if they were monkeys.

"Good," Evelyn said. "The FBI. Maybe you can tell me what the hell this has all been about."

"Mrs. Marshall, your name was bought to our attention as we were investigating a murder case in Falls Church," Chloe said

Evelyn levelled her eyes at her, her mouth set in a slant of annoyance. "Jessie Fairchild, I suppose?"

"That's right. How did you know about the murder?"

"News travels fast. I heard about it Friday afternoon."

"Were you surprised to hear about it?"

"That's hard to answer. On the one hand, it's terrible to think of someone in a neighborhood like that being killed. But on the other hand … no one liked her. I just wasn't aware that someone hated her enough to kill her."

"Did you—"

"I'm sorry," Evelyn said, raising her voice to make sure there was no mistake that she was intentionally cutting Chloe off. "Have I been detained from my flight because you actually think I'm a suspect?"

"We don't know any such thing yet," Chloe said. "What we *do* know is that you were involved in an altercation with her several days ago. And now, just a few days after her murder, you're leaving the country."

"Seems cut and dry to you, then? Is that how you work? The easiest solution *must* be the answer."

Chloe was beginning to grow tired of Evelyn's holier than thou attitude. Suddenly, the fact that she was handcuffed made her rather happy.

"This is a murder case, Mrs. Marshall," she said. "Believe it or not, there's *never* an easy answer. "But you *can* make it easier for us if you choose to do so. Can you tell us where you were last Friday morning?"

"I was actually in bed most of the morning. I wasn't feeling well. A migraine hit me the night before and they tend to linger."

"Do you get them often?" Rhodes asked.

"I do, in fact. It's linked to my TMJ."

"TMJ?" Chloe asked.

"Temporomandibular joint syndrome," Rhodes chimed in. "I get it from time to time, too. The joints in your jaw lock up."

"Exactly," Evelyn said. "And when my migraines hit, they usually last a day or two. I was in bed with that."

"Can anyone corroborate this?" Chloe asked.

"My nanny can. She took my son to the park for me so I could get some rest."

"Would you happen to have security cameras on your premises?" Chloe asked.

"I do. Why do you ask?"

"Because if we can get visual evidence that you never left your house Friday, you would be cleared."

To that point, Evelyn had been at least *pretending* to be civil. But something about that comment seemed to offend her. A hate-filled fire lit up in her eyes and she sat forward, as rigid as a set of prison bars.

"Cleared of what? Her murder? You two are absolutely precious…"

"I assume you won't give us your security footage then?" Rhodes asked.

"Hell no."

"That's fine," Chloe said. "We have enough just cause to issue a warrant for them. So we'll get them regardless."

"You do that. And also know that when this is all said and done, I fully intend to sue. I'll sue the airport for cuffing me and the FBI for sending you two to badger me about a murder you seem quite sure I committed when I have told you point-blank I was in my bed when the murder occurred."

"We're not sure of anything," Chloe said.

"Oh, that's obvious."

Chloe hated to admit it, but Evelyn had her rattled. The woman seemed so confident, so sure of herself. *Maybe always having money to bail you out of every uncomfortable situation creates that sort of confidence,* Chloe thought.

As she tried to find the best direction to take the interrogation, her phone buzzed in her pocket. She checked the caller ID and saw that it was Danielle. Her first instinct was to answer it, but that would be unprofessional. And God only knew Evelyn Marshall was looking for any further ammunition to support her cause.

She sent the call to voicemail and looked back to Evelyn Marshall. She could think of nowhere to go from here. It was clear she was going to be stubborn every step of the way.

"What do you take for your migraines?" Rhodes asked her.

Evelyn chuckled. "Trying to figure out if I know a thing or two about migraines, are you? Trying to make sure I'm not lying about them?"

The look on Rhodes's face made it clear that she, too, was tiring of Evelyn's little games.

When Chloe's phone rang in her pocket again, she was fuming. She checked the ID, saw that it was Danielle, and nearly sent it to voicemail again.

But then she thought of her apartment. She thought of how her father had destroyed it, how determined he had been to get that diary back. Maybe he paid Danielle a visit, too. Maybe she was calling because she was in danger.

"One second," Chloe said. "Sorry, I have to take this."

Rhodes looked at her with a bit of comical scorn. *Don't leave me with this woman alone,* that look seemed to say.

Chloe stepped out into the hallway and answered quickly as she closed the door behind her.

"Danielle, are you okay?"

There was a slight silence before Danielle answered. It made Chloe wonder if Danielle found that question an odd way to start a conversation.

"Chloe. Hey…"

"What's going on, Danielle."

"I need to talk to you," her sister said. Her voice was soft, something Chloe did not usually associate with Danielle's voice.

"Is it urgent?"

"Urgent... no. But—"

"Danielle, I'm glad you called and I want to patch things up. But this is the absolute worst time. I'm on a case in Falls Church and am right in the middle of questioning a suspect right now The timing is terrible."

"I'm sorry. I...I can call later."

"Are you in danger?"

"No. I'm fine. I just...I can talk to you later. You just...yeah. We'll talk later."

For a moment, Chloe thought she heard a slight tremor of emotion in Danielle's voice, as if she was on the verge of crying. Before she could say anything, though, Danielle ended the call. Chloe stared at her phone for a moment, her sibling instincts scattered all over the place.

She said she was fine, but she sure as hell didn't sound *fine.*

With a heavy feeling starting to press on her heart, Chloe had no choice but to pocket her phone. She walked back into the holding room where Evelyn Marshall continued to lash out at Rhodes. But even then, walking into that spoiled woman's tirade, Chloe's thoughts were stuck on Danielle.

CHAPTER NINETEEN

Chloe and Rhodes got back to the Falls Church PD just after 8:30. When they got there, Chloe spotted Chief Clifton, making only his second appearance since they had come into town to take the case. He looked pissed off, a scowl spread across his face as he approached them. They hadn't even made it three steps into the building before he stopped them. To his credit, he did not berate them or raise his voice. He did his best to remain quiet and civil. As he started, Chloe caught sight of Nolan not too far behind them eavesdropping on the conversation. He looked worried and a little amused. This relieved Chloe; apparently, he thought Clifton was all bark and no bite. He didn't seem to worried about their current predicament.

"I understand the need to speak with Evelyn Marshall," he said. "But did it have to be in such a confrontational way?"

"She made the conversation toxic," Chloe said. "She was defensive and pissy from the moment we walked in."

"Well, she *was* handcuffed," Clifton pointed out.

"Not by us. Airport security did that because she was endangering those around her."

"I just got off the phone with the head of security over there. He says she's talking about suing. And someone like Evelyn Marshall will do it. Even if it's just to cause trouble and stir the shit. Anything to make people see that you just don't fuck with her, plain and simple."

"Speaking of which," Chloe said, "we need a warrant for her security tapes from the Friday morning of Jessie Fairchild's murder."

"Ah, God," Clifton said.

"You really think she'd sue?" Rhodes asked. "Wouldn't it make her look petty?"

Clifton laughed. "Around here, the word *petty* tends to turn into *pity* a little too easy." He sighed and then turned away from them. Over his shoulder, he added: "I'll get started on getting that warrant for you."

It was one more deflating moment to tie off the evening— an evening that had already included having to speak to Evelyn Marshall and a strange phone call from Danielle. Chloe essentially slogged through the rest of the evening, sitting in the small conference room a while longer to go over the case files and the crime scene photos. She and Rhodes nearly decided to call Mark Fairchild to speak with him again but by then it was 9:25 and they felt there was no need to drag him through it all again at such an hour.

They left the building at 9:45 and headed home. There wasn't much talk between them on the way back into DC. The talk of suing everyone from Evelyn Marshall and then the passive-aggressive admonishments of Chief Clifton had taken their toll. Chloe personally didn't feel defeated yet but she felt like a boxer who had been battered and was basically leaning on the ropes for support.

Chloe and Rhodes went their own ways as they separated at FBI headquarters. Chloe drove home fighting the urge to call Danielle to see what she had wanted. But it was inching toward 10:30 and she didn't want to end the day on an emotionally draining note. She figured she could call her in the morning before she and Rhodes headed back into Falls Church.

She parked in front of her building and took the stairs up to her apartment. She felt like she might sleep well tonight, one of those sleeps that settle onto you like a cloud. She fumbled for her keys as she walked down the hallway.

She nearly dropped them when she saw Danielle standing outside her door.

Danielle looked at Chloe and her face crumpled. It was clear that she had been crying, but as her mouth drew into a straight line and went tight, she started again.

"Danielle?…"

But Danielle said nothing. Chloe met her sister at the door and wrapped her in an embrace as Danielle sobbed into her shoulder.

They went into the apartment and settled down on Chloe's couch. Danielle had already started to get control of herself, her crying tapering off to a series of little sobs. It was clear that she had already been crying for a good portion of the night; her eyes were red and her mascara had been running and wiped away.

"Talk to me, Danielle," Chloe said softly. "When you called, I asked if you were okay and you said you were fine."

"No, you asked if I was in danger. And I'm not."

"So what's wrong? If I'd known there was something this bad, I would have taken the call."

"I know. But I felt bad. I just can't ever get used to you having this super-important job where it's hard to get in touch with you."

"Well, I'm here now. What did you need to speak to me about? What's wrong?"

Chloe had never seen Danielle so shaken by something. It hurt her heart in a way she had not been expecting. She was dimly aware that her apartment was still slightly wrecked from the breaking and entering—from her father, coming in and rifling through her things for the journal.

"I made a mistake," Danielle said. "I made a really stupid mistake and I…I don't know if you can forgive me for it."

She couldn't help the first thought that crept into her mind.

What has she done to our father?

But just as quickly as it came to her, the thought vanished. Sure, Danielle had something of a dark side, but not *that* dark. At least, Chloe didn't think so.

"What did you do?" Chloe asked.

Danielle sniffed a sob back and picked up the small purse she had been carrying. Danielle rarely carried a purse, opting for a small backpack most of the time. It was the sort of small detail that made Chloe worry that something was indeed very wrong. She watched as Danielle reached into the purse and pulled out a small book—a book that was instantly familiar to Chloe.

It was her mother's diary.

At first, Chloe was too confused to react any certain way. But then a variety of possibilities began to dawn on her. None of them were particularly good.

"Danielle … how did you get that?"

Danielle swept her arm around the room as her head tilted down to the floor. "This was me," she said. "All of it. I did it. The break-in, trashing the place, stealing the journal."

Chloe instantly made herself get off of the couch. For a blinding moment, she had felt so angry and betrayed that she thought she might literally reach out and slap her sister hard across the face.

"And why did you do that?"

"Because I needed the journal. I needed to see … I needed to remember everything he had done."

"What the hell for?"

"I don't know. Chloe … you know now. You know the kind of man he was when you had your little blinders on and you're *not doing anything!*"

"Danielle … we could have just talked about this. You didn't have to do all of *this!*"

"I know. I figured if I trashed the place enough, you'd think it was him."

"Well, at least you succeeded in that …"

"Chloe, how can you be so passive? How can you not care?"

"Is that what you think? You think I don't care? Danielle, I'm sitting so tightly on it because we have to approach this just right. What the hell did you think I'd do? Just walk up and put a bullet in his head?"

"That would be better than doing nothing."

Frustration and rage flared through her as she paced back and forth, looking to Danielle with an emotion she wasn't even sure there was a name for.

"Tell me, Danielle. What is it that *you* would like to do?"

"You're the federal agent. Don't you have an in? Can't we get him locked up?"

"It's not quite that easy. We have to think about the way the system works. Double jeopardy won't allow him to be convicted of the same crime twice. The most that would come out of that would be putting him through the headache of court. Nothing more." She paused here and then wheeled on Danielle, as if starting the conversation afresh. "All that aside…what in God's name did you think you'd accomplish by breaking into my apartment? My neighbor heard you. If she's called the police a little earlier than she had, you could have gotten into some huge trouble. Don't you ever think about things like that?"

This seemed to bring Danielle around a bit. She finally managed to look up, locking eyes with her sister.

"I had to have it. It made it real for me…made me know for sure that I didn't just imagine it all—that I wasn't just imagining that Dad was such a bastard."

"We could have just talked about it…"

Chloe walked back to the couch and sat down. She was still enraged, but she could see the pain in Danielle's eyes. She could see traces of the little girl she had once been, a little girl who had witnessed the sort of monster their father truly had been—the sort of monster he very possibly still was.

"No, we couldn't. Chloe…are you sure you're not just delaying it? I tried asking you how you were feeling the other day and you made it pretty clear you didn't want to talk about it."

"Because I don't know what to talk about! I don't know what to do with it. I want to act on this…I truly do. But it has to be done right. The system…well, it sucks. There are so many loopholes and red tape…one misstep and he remains free."

"So what have you been doing?"

"I've been working a case, Danielle. I do still have a job. And you know what? Yes, I was glad to get the case. I was glad to have something to take my mind off of Dad and that damned journal. It was a great distraction from everything I've learned about him, from this horrible reality I have to face."

Danielle nodded. Chloe hoped she was understanding the one big unspoken comment that Chloe really didn't want to put words to—the fact that it had taken her so long to come to terms with the sort of man their father was. Neither of them wanted to speak out loud just how much Chloe had been wounded by all of this.

"So what do we do?" Danielle asked.

Chloe slumped against the couch. If she weren't so tired and if Danielle wasn't already so emotionally spent, this would have been a great night to kill a bottle of wine with her sister.

"This case I'm on is getting a little out of hand," Chloe said. "I can't give you details, obviously. But I have to finish it up. You let me finish this case and then you and I will work on this together. I'll open up—I'll talk to you and share what I know about how we could and could not effectively take it on. And when the time is right, we'll take it to the authorities."

"How long will that take?" Danielle asked.

"I don't know. This case could be wrapped tomorrow, or it could take another week or so. Maybe more. I just don't know. You need to be patient, Danielle. If we want him to get what he deserves, we have to do it the absolute right way."

"You're right," she said. "I know you are but I hate that fact that he's free. What stops him from just jumping to some other location?"

"I've thought of that, too. But he moved to DC for a reason. He wanted to be near us. At first I thought it was for sentimental reasons but now I think it's because he felt that we might pose some sort of threat."

"You think he knows that we know?"

"I don't know."

Danielle got to her feet and looked around at the mess, still clutching the journal. "Keep this. I'm still embarrassed that I did this to you. Here … let me clean up."

"Absolutely … but wait a day or so. It's clear that you've been dealing with this all day. You look drained, sis."

"I'm fine."

"I don't want you cleaning … not yet, anyway, but you're welcome to stay here tonight if you want."

Danielle thought about it for a moment before finally shaking her head. "No, I'm going to get back home. I just needed to see you. I had to get this all off my chest—had to confess to breaking into your place. I figured the entire time you'd think it was Dad and something about that started to feel sort of dirty, you know?"

"I get it. I just … well, I wish you and I were better at this sort of thing."

Danielle laughed as she headed for the door. "You're telling me." She took one final look around the apartment and frowned. "I really am sorry. Don't clean another thing. I'll come by tomorrow and do it."

"Sounds good. Goodnight, Danielle."

Danielle gave a tired little nod and slipped out the door.

Chloe sat down on the couch again and realized that in the drama, Danielle had ended up leaving with the journal. It made Chloe very uneasy, as if her sister had left with a loaded gun rather than a diary.

Chloe looked around the apartment, at the mess her sister—not her father—had made, and this time it was her turn to cry.

Chapter Twenty

The sudden twist in her personal life had resulted in poor sleep. Chloe's mind had been far too bogged down with trying to figure out how she could have been so blinded by her sudden distrust of their father. It was odd to think how just five months ago, she would never have suspected her father at all—and, as such, may have suspected Danielle right away.

Things seemed to be changing far too fast and it all started with her father. Or, more precisely, it started with her past feelings of adoration and love for her father. Even when they had been turned into feelings of anger and distrust, he was still clouding her judgment.

And then there was Danielle. The fact that she had actually broken into her apartment reminded Chloe far too much of the young woman her sister had once been: not subject to laws, a little on the dark side, no regard for the feelings of others.

Her mind felt like it had been set on fire, making it hard to sleep. She rested fitfully, managing about four hours of broken sleep. But when her eyes opened at 5:10, she knew she was done with sleep. There was just too much on her mind. She thought of her father and how he'd had her so fooled, how she had been so loyal and obedient to him. He'd played his part well, managing to fool her even though Danielle had always seen through him while their mother had taken on the brunt of his abuse.

It was just me, she thought. *I was the only one that never saw it.*

It was the first time the weight of this realization truly came down on her like a load of bricks. Perhaps that's why it suddenly triggered something in her head, something that temporarily cleared the fog of poor sleep.

She felt played—like she'd had the wool pulled over her eyes. She'd thought her father had been a good man, maybe a bit flawed by a few vices, but nothing like the revelations she'd come across as of late.

Almost idly, she thought of Mark Fairchild. He had a fairly airtight alibi, but not one that they had really thrown against the wall to see if it would stick. Even deep down in her guts, Chloe did not think he was guilty in any way. But, well, as the sleepless night had taught her, she sometimes failed to see the absolute evil in people if they hid it well enough.

She got out of bed, put on some coffee, and sat down at the kitchen table with the case notes. She looked over the little bit of information they had on Mark Fairchild and her instinct remained the same. She didn't see where he could have done it. There were at least five people that accounted for his whereabouts when his wife had been killed, as well as a receipt from a Panera Bread drive-through he went through just an hour and a half before she was killed.

But what if we dug deeper? she wondered. *These people were rich beyond measure. If you really wanted to unravel any secrets they were keeping, it would likely be buried under a lot of money.*

Chloe started making several notes, jotting them down on the margins of the printout they had on the Mark Fairchild interrogations. In the back of her mind, she was still tormented by questions and emotions concerning what Danielle had done, but she managed to push them away for the time being.

For now, she had to devote her full attention to the case—if not to bring a woman's murderer to justice, then for her own sanity.

Back in Falls Church, as Chloe and Rhodes started to truly dive deep into the personal lives of the Fairchilds, there seemed to be more and more evidence that there was no way Mark Fairchild had been in any way involved in the murder of his wife. Every single thing the police had asked for, he had willingly given. This included the alarm system codes, credit card information, bank statements, and full access to their computers and other electronic devices.

As it happened, this was incredibly helpful for what Chloe had planned as a start to their day. Nolan had everything she needed to dive deeper into the Fairchilds' finances already printed out and accurately organized. By 8:00 that morning, Chloe, Rhodes, and Nolan were sitting around the small conference room table in the back of the station, poring over the pages upon pages of financial records Nolan had printed out. There were a few that had not been printed that Nolan was able to access through banking websites and the log-in information Mark Fairchild had willingly given them.

The first thing that came to Chloe's attention was that there was an account set to the side, apart from savings and a 401k, that had been poured into for the last five years. To Chloe, it looked like nothing more than a secondary savings account—though, admittedly, she was not a banker and, in fact, she was easily annoyed with too much math and anything to do with numbers.

"Deputy Nolan, what do you know about this account?" she asked, circling the header indicating the account on one of the printouts. Nolan scooped the paper up, scanned it, and nodded.

"This is the retirement account he was telling us about."

Chloe looked at it again. "Any idea when Mark was planning to retire?"

"Next year. He's in the process of setting it all up right now. I hate to say it, but with his wife dying like this, when you add the life insurance to that account… it's going to be more than enough to retire on."

Again, it made Chloe wonder if Mark had something to do with Jessie's death. That nice chunk of change one year before he retired would certainly come in handy. But there was no evidence to support it.

"I keep coming back to this one little detail here," Nolan said. He was not looking at a printout, but at the laptop in front of him. Chloe and Rhodes walked over to his side of the table to look at the screen.

"What are we looking at?" Rhodes asked.

"Well, this column right here is their primary checking—an amount that makes me feel like I'm some commoner that's been eating scraps off of the streets, if I'm being honest. However, when you look at *this* column," he said, sliding his finger to the opposite side of the screen, "you see that a lot of it has been coming from transfers from a savings account. That's not all that unusual until you realize that they had never done anything like this up until about six months ago. And if you look at some of their expenditures and align it with these transfers from savings without putting anything else back *into* savings, it makes me wonder..."

"Was the money drying up?" Chloe asked, finishing his thought.

"Exactly. Of course, there's still seven hundred thousand dollars in their checking account, so I don't know if I'd say *drying up*. But when you consider that there was typically an account balance of at least three million with another five in savings, which is now down to under one million... that *is* where the trail starts to lead."

"Did he ever mention anything to you about financial problems when you got all of this information from him?" Rhodes asked.

"Nothing. How about you guys?"

"Nothing at all," Chloe said. "I'm looking at all of these transfers... they seem to be moved over to compensate for big expenditures. But the expenditures are either listed as simply withdrawals, other transfers, or checks that were written out. So we don't even know where all of that money was going."

"I noticed that, too," Nolan said. "And you know... I'll be honest... I never even thought much about it. I figured people with that much money must do some stupid things with it. He was so distraught over losing his wife I didn't even bother digging into it."

"That's understandable," Chloe said. "Given the situation, I would have probably done the exact same thing. But with no answers and the one potential break we have—Evelyn and a hair sample we're waiting to hear results on—we have to start looking *everywhere*."

"Want me to call Mark back in?" Nolan asked.

"I think it might be a good idea. Is he back at his home now?"

"As of yesterday, yeah...I think he's started arranging stuff for the funeral. He's a little upset that things have to be delayed because of the case."

"See if you can get him in," Chloe said. "The sooner the better."

"I'm sure he'll be accommodating," Nolan said. "He wants this nightmare over just as badly as we do."

Chapter Twenty One

The atmosphere wasn't quite as tense this time when Chloe and Rhodes sat down with Mark Fairchild. For one thing, his brother wasn't standing in a corner, listening in to the conversation. Also, while he was clearly still in the midst of his grieving, there seemed to be a platform of acceptance under all of Mark's emotions now. Chloe could see it simply in the way he was able to look back and forth between them as they spoke. He was clear-headed but still very much in pain.

"Thank you for coming back in," Chloe said. "I hated to ask for you to come back so soon, but quite frankly, we need some help."

"It's fine. Anything I can do ... I'm happy to do it. But first ... if I'm being honest ... can you tell me everything that's been cancelled out? I know you and the local PD were looking into several things, but what can you tell me has been ruled out?"

"Nothing much, regrettably," Chloe said. "But I can tell you things that we *know*. For instance, there were no prints on the fox stole or the ring other than your wife's. Along the way, we've also had some potential clues that have turned out to come to nothing. We do still have a few options open and if any of those turn out to be promising, we will certainly let you know."

He nodded, soaking all of the information in. He looked to the table, where they still had the majority of his financial records sitting out. "Can I assume the questions you have for me are related to finances?" he asked.

"That's correct," Rhodes said.

"Nothing incriminating by any means, of course," Chloe said. "But there were enough oddities to warrant another conversation with you."

"Sure." He sat back in his chair and looked a little nervous now. He had the look of a man that knew this had been coming—but maybe not quite so soon.

Chloe and Rhodes went through all of the discoveries they had made. Both of them were very careful to not sound as if they were accusing him of anything. They spoke to him with the interest of two agents simply needing more information. It seemed to set him a bit more at ease. Chloe had seen this tactic work before; rather that feeling cornered, he felt helpful. It was a surefire way to get someone to slip up if they were, indeed, hiding something.

When they were done showing him what led them to needing his help, he gathered up all of the papers in question and stared at them for a moment. He stacked them into a neat little pile and looked down at them introspectively.

"I know it's not very modern or *woke* or whatever the hell people would call it, but Jessie was never really aware of what was going on financially. The last time she even showed any sort of interest in where we were financially was about a year and a half ago. We had seventeen million dollars broken up between a few accounts, I had some stocks valued at over five million, and about another ten million in savings. She asked casually how we were financially one more time when we knew we had to move, but that was it. I was always the one that managed the money, balanced everything, and so on. She just… well, she spent quite a bit of it. And I don't say that to be pissy because she didn't keep it secret, made sure I was fine with it all. I just asked that if she wanted anything that was over a certain amount, to let me know first."

"And what was that amount?" Chloe asked.

"Twenty thousand."

"When was the last time she asked to go over that amount?" Rhodes asked.

"It's been a while. Two months, maybe?"

"Did it ever cause arguments between the two of you?"

"No, nothing serious. It's … well, it all seems stupid now, but I never minded her spending money. I was always about keeping her happy. And after a while, you become dependent on the money. I think we made each other happy emotionally and physically but at the end of the day, we both got very used to having all of the money, you know? But now that she's gone, the money really doesn't amount to much as far as I'm concerned."

"It sounds like she might have been more frivolous with the money than you were," Chloe pointed out.

"Oh, she was at times. And that's not me talking about her while she's not here to defend herself. If she was still here, she'd tell you the same thing."

"All of the things we discovered this morning … well, it led us to some conclusions that we aren't really professionally trained to make. Care you weigh in?"

"You're trained enough, it seems," Mark said with a frown. "Yeah, we were bleeding money. I wouldn't quite say we were going broke, but if things didn't change soon, I might have had to consider filing for bankruptcy."

"Where was all of the money going?"

"I don't know how to answer those questions without boring you. It's all in investments. If you need me to, I can have someone at the office dig into the accounts and provide printouts for you."

"I don't think that will be necessary just yet, but we may need to come back to it eventually."

Mark seemed relieved about this, but it was clear that it was still hard for him to talk about it. "Some of it was invested in a club that a friend of mine was opening up in New York. He ended up owing money to some other people and went under. I never saw the money back and I don't even know where he disappeared to. Some of the other money I sort of pissed away on a gambling problem that Jessie never even knew about. I hit one big win at the races last year and got hooked."

"Anything else?" Chloe asked. She had a decent sense for when someone was withholding something from her and while she knew it was hard for Mark to share the things he had told them so far, she felt like there might be something else.

"I can't... it's too hard," he said, essentially confirming this.

"This is private information, Mr. Fairchild. If it has nothing to do with your wife's murder, it doesn't have to leave this room."

"It's ... well, it's not my proudest moment. There was ... a day two years ago when I left for a trip overseas. I went to Tokyo for three weeks. I had too much to drink one night and ended up going home with an escort. A very pricey escort. And I just... I hate to say it, but I got hooked. I hired her two more times the following year—flying her out over here both times. And then she moved to New York last year and asked me if I would be interested in her and a friend at once. Of course, the price was higher..."

"How much money are we talking?" Chloe asked, fully aware once the question was out of her mouth that she really had no business asking.

"I'd rather not say," he said, quickly glancing to the printouts in front of him. "It's... deplorable. Embarrassing."

"Dumb question here," Rhodes said. "But did your wife ever know about this?"

"No."

With that, he hung his head and let out a massive sob.

Chloe and Rhodes shared a look across the table. There was guilt in that glance but there was also an unspoken discovery: Mark Fairchild was fully capable of keeping secrets.

And if he had been able to keep these secrets from his wife, what other secrets might he be capable of keeping so closely guarded?

Mark Fairchild left the police station fifteen minutes later, assuring Chloe and Rhodes that he held no ill feelings toward them. These were his own stupid sins after all, he had said, and he had to deal with them in a whole new light now that Jessie was no longer with him. He left the agents alone in the small conference room once again, now with a new round of questions hovering between them.

"What do you think?" Rhodes asked. It was a simple question, but was also a very heavy one, loaded with all sorts of possibilities.

"I think he's torn up about the escorts—that it hurt more than he realized to actually admit it. But I also know that a man that lies about one thing is very prone to lie about much more. How about you?"

"I think we need to look deeper into him. He's losing money on these dumb decisions he's made and he needed more money. By killing her, I think he eliminates an unnecessary money suck while also cashing in on her considerable life insurance policy."

"That's where I was initially headed, too. But his alibi is too tight. Five people have been interviewed and can voice for his whereabout the entire time."

"I know. But you seem to be forgetting the man is loaded. If he can blow ungodly amounts of money on expensive foreign prostitutes, he can likely hire someone to kill his wife."

"That's a big assumption to make without any evidence to support it."

"I agree," Rhodes said. There was a tone of defensiveness to her voice as she reached onto the table and fanned out the printouts. "But we have several large transactions in this financial history that are unaccounted for. I think if we really dig into them, we might find some answers."

Chloe considered it for a moment but then shook her head. It simply didn't feel right. "If he did indeed pay someone to kill his wife—which I find highly unlikely, by the way—you're not going to find the transaction in his bank records. No one would be that stupid … especially not someone that keeps a tight eye on his finances."

"Yeah, but any of these transactions that are simple withdrawals of cash … there's no telling what he could have done with the money."

"Exactly. He admitted he has a gambling issue and it isn't anything out of the ordinary for him to hire prostitutes. So just assuming any cash withdrawals were used to pay someone to kill his wife is a stretch."

A frown worked its way across Rhodes's face. "I mean this with the utmost respect," she said, "but I find it weird that you aren't at least considering this. It's not like we're drowning in answers."

"That's true. But I'm not about to accuse a man who just lost his wife of said wife's murder without sufficient reason to do so."

"I just gave you the reasons, Chloe."

"And it's my opinion that they aren't nearly strong enough to warrant us openly investigating Mark Fairchild."

Something a bit more sinister than a frown crossed Rhodes's face in that moment. She shook her head, shrugged indignantly, and got up from the table. She made no effort to hide the fact that she was pissed off when she exited the room.

Chloe took the moment of silence to lean back in her chair and truly wonder why she was so opposed to putting poor Mark Fairchild through the investigation. She was well aware that there were a few curious marks against him, though not enough, in her opinion, to point to him as a likely suspect.

It was more than a gut instinct. It was something else she couldn't quite pinpoint—something she was pretty sure was directly linked to her own life. It occurred to her that Mark Fairchild was essentially in the same position her father had been in almost ten years ago: with a recently killed wife, with the authorities starting to suspect him as the killer.

Maybe that's why I'm so insistent that Mark isn't the killer, she thought. *Maybe it feels too personal.*

Another thought followed this one, this thought coming to her in Danielle's voice. *Yeah*, she said. *And you were wrong about that one at the start…*

As she mulled this over, there was a knock at the door. Nolan poked his head in. The look on his face made it quite clear that he was not delivering the best news.

"Any news?" Chloe asked.

"Yeah, but it's all eliminating your leads. The officers I had check over Evelyn Marshall's security tapes found that she was telling the truth. She never left her house on the morning Jessie Fairchild was killed. She went out to water her rosebushes around nine thirty and that's it. Also … the hair sample … we just got the call from forensics. It's not Evelyn's. In fact, they think it's pretty likely that it was from a male. They have to run more tests to be certain, but that seems to be the case."

"Evelyn has been released, then?"

"Yeah. And still screaming about suing us."

"I doubt she will. Her type is all bark and no bite. Being involved in anything legal would smear her reputation."

"I was thinking the same thing."

"Thanks for the update."

"Sure. Hey … is everything okay? I saw Rhodes out in the hallway a few minutes ago and she looked like she was fuming about something."

Yeah, Chloe thought. *And that's likely my fault.* Instead, she said: "She's fine. No answers, no real leads … it's getting to us."

Nolan nodded his understanding and said, "Let me know what I can do to help," as he headed back out of the room.

Chloe got to her feet and headed out as well. She had no clear destination in mind, but she needed to feel like she was moving, like she was making *some* kind of progress. Second by second, she started to feel that she was in the wrong with Rhodes. Of course they needed to dig into Mark a bit deeper. The trick was making sure she could get out of her own way—to set her own demons aside and focus on the ones that mattered.

CHAPTER TWENTY TWO

Chloe had never been the best when it came to asking for help. It had been true when she'd been a child, had gotten worse as she'd evolved into a teen, and had become something of a defining trait when she had entered adulthood. From needing help with courses in college to breaking down on the side of the road when her first car had called it quits, she had always hesitated to ask for help.

That's why it felt so strange for her to sit alone in the bureau car she had shared with Rhodes over the last few days, take out her cell phone, and stare at the phone number that she had called only once. She had been so certain she would never call it again that she had not bothered saving it as a contact.

She'd gotten the number of Dr. Fischer immediately after she had booked Ruthanne Carwile for her part in her mother's murder. She wasn't even quite sure who had given it to her—it had probably been Johnson—and she honestly hadn't thought of Fischer in over two months.

Dr. Robin Fischer specialized as a behavioral therapist but was also tied to the bureau in that she helped agents who had recently been through traumatic experiences and were having trouble processing. The two sessions Chloe had participated in had been forced and awkward, but, as much as she hated to admit it, they had helped her process through a lot of unidentified grief and anger she had pent up ever since finding her mother's dead body at the age of ten.

And now here she was again, finding herself bogged down by her past—by her father and her inability to let go of the man he had once been and the crimes that had been committed by the man he *truly* was.

Approaching thirty, it was time to face the fact that it was not something she was going to be able to release on her own. With a deep sigh, she called the number on the screen. Her heart seemed to cringe at the two rings on the other end before it was answered.

"Dr. Fischer's office," a soft friendly voice said.

"Hi. This is Agent Chloe Fine, with the FBI. I was wondering if Dr. Fischer had any availability today for a quick phone conversation."

"Let me see," the friendly voice said. She then made a series of cute humming noises as the clicking of a mouse could also be heard. Chloe assumed she was looking through Fischer's calendar.

"I'm not sure, actually," the receptionist voice responded. "The only thing she has is at the end of the day. Would that work for you?"

Chloe felt a little relieved. Fischer would call back at the end of the day and by then, Chloe would be over the need to speak to someone. Bullet effectively dodged.

"No, that's okay."

"Are you sure?"

"Yes, thanks," Chloe said, hanging up before the receptionist could press further.

She peered into the rearview, looking at the Falls Church police department. Rhodes was still in there somewhere, probably thinking that she, Chloe, was being a stubborn bitch. And honestly, Chloe figured she *was* being a stubborn bitch. Now she had to explain herself *and* apologize. Both of which would be just as hard as having a conversation with Dr. Fischer.

Apparently, she had not dodged that bullet after all.

She reached for the door handle to head back inside to look for Rhodes but was stopped by the ringing of her phone. When she saw that it was the very number she had just called, she almost didn't answer it.

Wow, I really didn't dodge that bullet, she thought.

Resigned to the conversation ahead, she answered. "This is Agent Fine."

"Agent Fine, this is Dr. Fischer. I'm told you just called looking for some time to speak. I have about ten minutes right now. Would that work? Of course, if you need something more extensive, we can schedule an in-office visit."

"Ten minutes is fine. Maybe too long."

"Well, typically, I would have just let a call go. But when I was told it was you who called, I wanted to reach out. I heard about your father getting released, after all. Can I assume that's what this is about?"

"In a roundabout way, yes. He's moved to DC, less than three miles from my apartment. And I've recently discovered some things about him…about his past. I can't get the bastard out of my thoughts and I fear it's beginning to affect my work."

"In what ways?" Fischer asked.

"It's hard to explain. I'm unconsciously applying my prior feelings towards him to this current case I'm working on."

"Well, the fact that you're aware of it means that it's not *totally* unconscious. I think you're very aware it's what you're doing but are failing to face it."

It was a harsh comment, quite hard to hear but Chloe knew it was the truth. "Is that normal?"

"It depends on what you consider normal," Fischer said.

"I don't even know how to answer that."

"Answer *this* then: do you want to face it? Deep down, in your heart of hearts, are you afraid of facing the idea of doing away with your father? You said you have discovered some things about him recently, so I assume they're quite bad things. Does this new knowledge carry as much weight as all of those years you spent adoring him and trying to defend him?"

"Not at first," she said, not even realizing the truth of it until it was out of her mouth. She almost came out and revealed some of the things she had discovered—about her mother's journal and the secrets it revealed. But in the end, she kept it to herself, not wanting to get into the implications of telling her therapist about such a potential bomb blast. Instead, she simplified things by adding: "But it's starting to take over."

"So it's safe to say there's something of a war going on inside your mind and your heart. Would you agree?"

A bit cheesy, Chloe thought but yes, she did agree. "I suppose," she answered.

"Well, the good news with that is that *you* get to decide which side wins."

"I figured it should be easier than this, though."

"Regrettably, it never is with family. Especially in a situation like you're looking at. Look, I hate to push you off, but I do have an appointment that starts in three minutes. Do you want me to book you some time next week to come in?"

"Thanks, but I don't think so."

"I'm going to reserve a block for you next Monday," Fischer said. "I'll just pencil it in. If you don't show up, no big deal. How does that sound?"

"That's fine," Chloe said, even though the thought of sitting in that office and spilling her guts again terrified her.

"Take care, Agent Fine. And don't hesitate to call me if you need anything else."

They ended the call and this time, Chloe was able to get out of the car uninterrupted. As she did, she was able to rest a bit easier thanks to one single comment Dr. Fischer had made: *The good news with that is that you get to decide which side wins.*

She headed back to the building, fully aware that she needed to find Rhodes and let her know that she was likely right—that they needed to dig deeper into Mark Fairchild.

Because the closer she got to the door, she started to slowly understand one very strange set of circumstances that she had either totally missed or conveniently overlooked.

Mark had all but admitted that yes, they had slowly been going broke. He had been fully aware of this. Yet, at the same time, he was still planning to retire in the next few years. How would he do that much planning unless he knew something might change?

It was so obvious that it was almost jarring.

And it had Chloe increasing her speed as she neared the front door, now rather anxious to let Rhodes know she might have been right all along.

CHAPTER TWENTY THREE

Chloe found Rhodes in Nolan's office. She was looking over several printouts, scanning them meticulously. Chloe wasn't surprised to see that they were the same financial documents they had been looking over earlier. Rhodes looked up from the paper, gave a curt little nod, and then turned her attention back to the paper.

"Agent Rhodes, can I speak with you for a moment?" Chloe asked, trying to sound as professional as possible in front of Nolan.

Before Rhodes could answer, Nolan stood up from his chair and plopped down the folder he had been thumbing through. "Use the office," he said. "I need to make a visit to the coffee pot, anyway."

Nolan got up and left the room. Rhodes slowly set her paper down and looked to Chloe, clearly not sure what to expect. This had been their first difference of opinion on pretty much anything ever since Chloe had saved her life after getting shot on their first case together. It made for an odd feeling between the two.

"I'm not going to go deep into it," Chloe said, "but you're right. We should be looking into Mark Fairchild. There's … well, there are just some things going on in my personal life that are clouding my judgment. Do with that what you will … but I *am* sorry. I do think you're right, though. Mark Fairchild needs to be considered not only a suspect, but a likely one."

"What brought you around?"

"The fact that he knew they were going broke *and* let his wife continue to spend money like it was going out of style while *also* planning to retire in the next few years. That doesn't add up. It makes me think he had been planning for some way out."

"Yeah, I keep sticking to that theory, too," Rhodes said.

Just like that, the rift between them was mended. A brief silence passed between them as Chloe looked down at the stack of papers. "We don't have a copy of Jessie's life insurance policy, do we?"

Rhodes grinned while shaking her head. "No. Not yet, anyway. I called right after I left the room to request a copy."

"Do we know how much she was covered for, at least?" Chloe asked.

"Nolan said that during his first conversation with Mark, it came up. Mark seemed unsure of the total, but said he thought it landed somewhere in the neighborhood of two million."

"That's insane. I wonder if that's typical for rich people."

"Throw a rock in their neighborhood and ask whoever it hits," Rhodes commented. "Anyway, Nolan and I were just working on getting a few officers to go back to the Fairchild residence and go over the whole house again. We're pulling his phone records, too. Mark has already offered his bills, which have a list of all calls made, but we're going deeper."

"That's what confuses me," Chloe said.

"What's that?"

"That Mark Fairchild is being very open and transparent. He's allowing us into his house, he's offering up information willingly. He's either very good at hiding things or he's innocent."

"He hid expensive prostitutes from him wife," Rhodes pointed out. "And a pretty severe gambling problem."

"Touché."

They both reverted back to silence, only this time they were both deep in thought, taking the thread in their own directions. Chloe knew that if she could simply get into the mind of the killer, she could better determine if Mark Fairchild was capable of killing. She did her best to remove jealousy from the equation…because when she got right down to it, she didn't think any of the women in the Fairchild's neighborhood or other neighboring areas would actually commit murder. There was simply too much to lose: reputation, good standing, flawlessly fake façade and all. Even someone like Evelyn Marshall, as evil as she seemed, would always choose stature and wealth over vengeance.

When jealousy or pettiness was removed, it allowed for more primal things—more basic urges and desires. A woman, new to the neighborhood, could be the target of many different type of men (and, she supposed, women as well).

"The women in the neighborhood had everything to lose," Chloe said out loud. "Killing someone ... they'd lose everything if they found out. They'd have everything to lose by committing murder. But Mark ..."

"Mark had something to gain," Rhodes finished up. "Namely that big fat life insurance policy. And you know, Nolan said that the reporters have officially started to knock on Mark's door. Sucks for him, sure, and the reporters are scum, but if he *is* hiding something, he can only talk to but so many people before he slips up somehow."

Nolan appeared in the doorway, as if summoned by the mention of his name. He sipped from his newly filled mug of coffee, nodding along. "Reporters are calling here, too. Wanting to details, like we'd actually give them anything."

"We need the details of that life insurance policy," Chloe said. "How long before we get a copy?"

"Should be any minute now. But you know, I was thinking it over in the break room just now. Seeing the policy itself isn't going to really matter. All you really need to do is call up the Fairchilds' insurance agent and see if the policy had been changed or altered recently."

"Nolan, you're a genius," Rhodes said.

"I do what I can."

"The name of the company and the agent were in the case overview, right?" Chloe asked, already fishing for it. "Right here."

She slid the information over to Rhodes, silently furthering her apology by non-verbally letting her partner know that she deserved the credit for pushing through toward this line of reasoning. It was a humbling feeling and, quite frankly, not one that she cared to feel again. Rhodes took the paper, placed her finger under the number, and put Nolan's desk phone on speaker. She dialed in the number and the three of them stood as still as statues as they listened to the phone ringing on the other end.

It was answered after the first ring by a young-sounding woman. "Ideal State Insurance," she said. "This is Tammy."

"Tammy, this is Agent Nikki Rhodes with the FBI. I need to speak with Brian Everson, please."

"I'm sorry, but Mr. Everson is with a client. Can I have him call you back?"

"No, Tammy, you can't. Again ... this is the FBI. I need to speak with Brian Everson concerning a life insurance policy and it is incredibly urgent. I need to speak to him right now, please."

"Of course," Tammy said, clearly spooked by the forceful yet polite tones Rhodes had used to get what she wanted.

There was an audible click on the line as they were placed on hold.

"This Everson guy is one of the most popular insurance salesmen in the area," Nolan said. "He seems like a legitimately great guy. I don't think we'll have any problems with getting the information we need."

Roughly one minute passed before the line was picked back up. The voice on the other end was now male, and sounded a little concerned. "This is Brian Everson ... can I help you?"

"Mr. Everson, my name is Nikki Rhodes, and I'm a field agent with the FBI. We're in Falls Church to look into the murder of one of your clients, Jessie Fairchild. We've put in a request for a copy of her life insurance policy, but are in a bit of a rush. Can you pull up her file right now, with us on the phone?"

"Giving that sort of information over the phone is unorthodox," Everson said. "How am I supposed to know you're actually an agent? Do you know how much gossip and turmoil has come about because of this murder?"

Rhodes gave the phone an annoyed look. "Grab a sheet of paper, Mr. Everson. I'll give you my badge number and the direct line to my supervisor. If you need to call him, go right ahead."

BLAKE PIERCE

"Just for the sake of covering myself, give me both, would you?"

Rhodes, clearly irritated, gave Everson her badge number as well as the number to Johnson's office—which she had to get from her own phone.

"Okay, so what exactly are you looking for?" Everson asked.

"We just need to know if the policy had been altered in any way in the past year or so."

There was the sound of someone typing into a computer for a few moments before Everson came back on the line. "Of course, they just moved into town, so what I am looking at is coming directly from their previous agent—also an agent with Ideal State. I can see that the policy is about fifteen years old. And from what I can see here, there's nothing that has been changed lately. There's an increase in coverage from six years ago, but nothing else."

"And can you tell me if it's common for life insurance policies to be so large for wealthier families?"

"I wouldn't say it's common, but it does happen."

"Can you tell us what the payout for this particular policy would be?"

"A little more than three million."

Chloe, Rhodes, and Nolan all shared a look of disbelief.

"But you're certain there have been no changes recently?" Rhodes asked. "Nothing that might make the policy a little ..."

"Advantageous?" Everson asked. His voice was hushed, almost like he was telling a deep, dark secret.

"That would be a good word."

"No. I actually had a look at the policy yesterday. Mr. Fairchild came by to go over it and when I tried to explain some of the standard procedures to him, he shook his head and dismissed himself."

"Angry?" Rhodes asked.

"No. He was doing everything he could not to start crying right in front of me."

Rhodes hesitated for a moment and then shrugged. "Thanks for your help, Mr. Everson."

She ended the call and then looked back to the stack of papers on Nolan's desk. The room was quiet for a moment—so quiet that Chloe could almost hear the potential for such a strong lead starting to crumble.

"Okay, so maybe it's not him," Rhodes said. "I was so sure there was *something* going on."

"Keep in mind, he's got all of those other bank accounts, too," Chloe pointed out. "He could be hiding something in those."

"We've looked into that, though," Nolan said. "Jessie wasn't directly tied to any of those accounts."

"Still, it's entirely possible that he could have—"

Chloe was interrupted by a knock on the door. Chief Clifton poked his head into Nolan's office, still knocking as he did so. A look of fury was on his face, his eyes narrowed and his cheeks going red.

"Nolan…did Mark Fairchild mention this press conference bullshit to you?"

"Press conference?" Nolan asked, speaking the word as if he had never heard it before. "What?"

"So I guess that's a no."

"What press conference?" Rhodes asked.

"He's about to go on TV, at his house, with a shit-ton of reporters. I think he got flanked and decided now was better than never."

"Without a police presence?" Nolan asked.

"Stupid, I know," Clifton said. "Sherry has it on the TV in the bullpen."

The four of them quickly left Nolan's office, headed down the hallway, and joined five others in the bullpen. The small flat-screen sat on top of an older-looking desk, flanked by several folders and a laptop. On the screen, Mark Fairchild could be seen standing on his large porch, huddled with another man and speaking in private. Off of the porch, several reporters were jockeying for position. There was no mic or podium for Mark, just the stage of his front porch.

"Who is that he's conferring with?" Chloe asked.

Nolan made a chuffing noise as he sneered at the television. "That's Kenneth Holt, a pretty big-name lawyer."

"How the hell did this become such a media circus so fast?" Rhodes asked.

"A few reporters had pinged us, like I said," Nolan answered. "But I guess more than we knew were contacting Mark. But he never told me anything about it."

Seems a little strange, Chloe thought. *Is he soaking up the attention for a reason other than wanting to feel loved or supported?*

They watched for another two minutes as Mark and Kenneth Holt finished up their discussion. The gathering of reporters and news crews was small, no more than three crews total if Chloe was counting right. Finally, Mark walked to the edge of his porch, where the stairs started. He looked down to the gathered crowd with a resigned and fake smile.

"This is going to be short," he said. "I wanted to just put some sort of word out there so reporters would stop calling or hunting me down. I need time to grieve, but apparently that sort of thing just isn't allowed these days."

There were no grumbles of argument from the news crews he was speaking to. Chloe doubted they were even listening; they were too focused on getting the right shot and angle.

"There are still no solid leads in finding my wife's killer," Mark went on. "The Falls Church PD has been incredibly helpful and are working hard, in tandem with the FBI. But as of now, we have no answers. I am also painfully aware that there are theories floating around that I personally killed my wife for the insurance money. This thought saddens and sickens me in equal measure. But to put that stupid theory to rest, I will be donating every penny of the money that comes from the life insurance towards several charities that were near and dear to Jessica's heart."

This did get a few murmurs from the reporters. Someone tried asking a question, but Mark was having none of it. He spoke his next words loudly and with a bit of anger behind them. "For now, these are the only statements I will be making. I continue to ask that all media outlets leave me alone. Any further disturbances will be met with legal action and I have no problem with calling the police. Thank you."

With that, Mark turned away from the crowd and joined Holt back by the door, Holt opened the front door and they both disappeared inside. The news feed, of course, remained on the image of the closed door for quite some time.

"Well, that was ballsy," Nolan said.

"It was," Chloe agreed. "And I'm sure he thinks what he just did is going to make things easier for him, but I think he's going to be sorely disappointed."

"How so?" Nolan asked.

"On the surface, it seems selfless and maybe noble. From an investigative standpoint, it seems like he's pretty anxious to get rid of that money."

"I'm not sure I follow," Chief Clifton said.

"I don't completely follow it myself," Chloe said. "Not yet, anyway."

She checked her watch and saw that it was already 5:15. She had no idea how it had gotten so late so fast. "Has anyone bothered checking his office?" she asked.

"There were two laptops that he willingly handed over," Nolan said. "It was the only thing he's willingly done that he seemed a little weird about. But I figured he had a right to feel that way, given everything he's gone through."

"Any idea how long the offices are open?"

"According to Mark, there are usually people there until midnight or so. People come and go after six in the evening, based on the level of projects or deals that are going down."

"The laptops ... did he give them to you or were they confiscated?"

"He gave them up on his own. Gave me the key to his office without a problem."

"You still got that key?"

"I do, actually. In the craziness that's been going down these last few days, I don't think he ever even bothered to ask for it back."

To a layman, Chloe thought this might be further proof that Mark Fairchild had nothing to hide. That or it could be a genius front.

"Mind if we borrow it?" Chloe asked.

"Not at all. Let me grab it for you."

Nolan headed back to his office as Clifton drifted back into the bullpen and toward his own office, located near the back. This left Chloe and Rhodes alone again, finally back on the same track.

"What are you thinking?" Rhodes asked. "Maybe he was hiding something in his office?"

"I think it's worth a shot. He's been too easily handing over information and now he's making a public declaration that he's going to give all of the life insurance money away. There's *being helpful* and then there's just *entirely too convenient*. And right now ... I get a weird feeling about it all."

"It doesn't help that Nolan said Fairchild got antsy when offering up his work laptops."

Before Chloe could comment on this, Nolan was headed back toward them. He tossed Chloe a key, which she deftly caught with one hand. She pocketed it, gave her thanks, and headed for the door.

Maybe it was because she felt she had been duped by Mark Fairchild's helpfulness and grief—or maybe it was just because this damned case seemed to have no viable leads anywhere in sight. But for some reason, as she and Rhodes headed for the door, Chloe felt the stirrings of motivation deep in her gut. It was more than a motivation to bring the case to a close, though. It was more like a drive and determination to expose some secrets ... to bring the darkness into the light and absolutely obliterate it.

Chapter Twenty Four

Danielle had meant every word she'd said when she visited Chloe yesterday. She deeply regretted trashing Chloe's apartment and was ashamed that she had stooped so low as to stealing the journal away from Chloe. While she had been at her sister's apartment, there had been a moment before leaving when she had nearly tossed the journal onto Chloe's coffee table. It would have been the responsible thing to do. But in the end, she had held onto it and Chloe had not bothered to ask for it back.

That's how the journal was still with Danielle, sitting in the fork of her legs as she sat behind the wheel of her car. It was dark, and the rows of townhouses in front of her loomed high up into the night sky.

She stared out at one of the townhouses in particular. Weak white light filtered out through the window along the front. A few townhouses further down, a streetlight illuminated most of the front stoop.

It occurred to her then that the stairs to her father's new townhouse looked a great deal like the front stoop she and Chloe had been sitting on when the authorities had been inside their parents' old apartment, looking over the dead body of their mother. With a crooked smile, Danielle grabbed her mother's diary and stepped out of the car. She walked to her father's townhouse feeling surprisingly calm.

She'd only decided about an hour ago that she was going to do this. It seemed simple, so simple that she wasn't sure why she hadn't done it yet. But when the idea had come to her, it had reminded her of something—of some dark time, of perhaps something she had been forgetting.

Undaunted, she'd gotten into her car with the diary and now here she was—slowly walking up her father's steps. She was almost made uneasy by how calm she felt. She'd expected to feel frightened or nervous or…or *something*. But there was nothing. If anything, there was a feeling of *why haven't I already done this?*

She approached his door and knocked on it without much thought. She stepped back and waited. She *did* feel a slight pang of nervousness when she heard the lock being released, but it was fleeting. When the door was opened and she saw her father standing in front of her, it did not rattle her the way she had been expecting.

Aiden Fine, on the other hand, *did* look rattled. His eyes went wide for a moment and she thought he might actually slam the door in her face. But after a moment had passed, he tried on a smile and took a step back.

"Danielle … hello, dear."

"Hey, Dad," she said. "Do you … well, do you have a second?"

"Of course," he said. But his tone indicated that he wasn't so sure about this. Still, he stepped back further to allow her inside. "Is everything okay?" he asked as she stepped past him and he closed the door.

"No. Things aren't okay."

"Can I help with something?" he asked.

Danielle did not answer right away. Instead, she let him lead her into his place. He opted for the kitchen, which was the first room the small entryway led into. He leaned against the counter, clearly nervous, as she stepped in. He opened his mouth to say something else but then saw what his daughter was holding in her hands.

"Where'd you get that?" he asked. His tone was not an accusing one, but one of absolute fear.

"Wouldn't you like to know," she said. "Have you read it?"

"Some of it," he said. He was slowly beginning to calm down. She could see him thinking, trying to decide which was the best approach to take here.

As for Danielle, she moved just slightly to the left. She stepped deeper into the kitchen in front of his stove. She found it peculiar in a way that he had salt and pepper shakers, a tea kettle, a little utensil rack next to the stove. Who the hell did he think he was, trying to be normal?

"You want to try explaining yourself?" she asked. "Not that you have to. I always knew you were an abusive piece of shit. The adultery stuff was new, though—the stuff Chloe and I discovered about you recently."

"Your mother was dramatic," he said. "I know she wrote about how she feared I might kill her. How I—"

"I'm not Chloe, Dad. I never had blinders on, so you can cut that nonsense right now. I just want to hear you say it."

"Say what?"

"You know what I want to hear. I want you to tell me the truth." That said, she tossed the diary on the counter. Her father looked at it as if someone had thrown a grenade at him. But slowly, he reached for it.

"Need a refresher, do you?" Danielle asked.

"Danielle, you have to give me a chance—"

"No . . . no I don't."

"None of what is in here is how it sounds. You have to believe me."

Danielle said nothing. Slowly, she leaned away from the counter, very aware of the space behind her—of the stove and all of the things sitting out on it. She watched as her father took the diary in his hands and that's when she moved.

She moved quickly. She reached behind her, grabbed the tea kettle, and swung around in a vicious arc. Her father saw what was coming, but far too late. His face went rigid in the last moment, knowing what was coming. Danielle wasn't sure what amused her more: the look of knowing there was pain coming, or the absolute and utter shock in his eyes.

The kettle slammed into the side of his head and made a sound that was almost like something out of a cartoon. Aiden stumbled back into the counter and by the time he had his senses about him,

Danielle swung the kettle again. This time, the sound it made as it connected with his cheek was not cartoonish at all. There was a cracking noise that seemed to vibrate within the kettle.

The shot dropped Aiden Fine to his knees. He fought for balance but then fell over, his eyes in a dreamlike haze. He grasped for Danielle's leg to get up, letting out a moan of pain.

Danielle looked him in the eyes. She smiled and then raised the kettle again. This time, she brought it down hard against the back of his head. The *bong* sound it made was like some sweet percussion that rattled her hand.

Aiden's grip on her leg was released at once as he dropped face-down to his kitchen floor. As carefree as you please, Danielle tossed the tea kettle across the kitchen, where it bounced into the living room.

She leaned down to check his pulse and when she was certain he was still alive and breathing, she quickly searched his house. It took her about five minutes to find everything she needed. Packed away in the back of the bedroom closet, she found a large quilt, still in its plastic wrapping and likely never used. He'd apparently purchased it on sale, waiting for colder temperatures to use it. She carried it into the kitchen and spread it out. She then rolled her father onto it. When she did, he muttered something under his breath that made her aware that maybe he wasn't as knocked out as she had thought. She quickly did her best to fold the quilt over him, realizing how stupid of an idea it was. But, because it was the only one she had, she stuck with it.

She found duct tape in a junk drawer on the right side of the kitchen. When she started wrapping it around the blanket, doing her best to cover as much of his body as possible, he stirred again. She used the tea kettle once more, again blasting him on the back of the head. For a moment, she feared this blow had killed him, but rested easy when she saw the subtle rise and fall of his chest beneath the quilt.

She finished wrapping the tape around the quilt and saw how obvious the shape beneath the quilt was. Fortunately, it was night outside. And her car was only two spaces away from his front door.

She walked to the door and opened it. There was a single person on the little concrete strip along the front of the townhouses—a woman walking her golden retriever. She watched and waited until the woman was gone and then saw her chance. She grabbed her keys from her pocket and used the remote to pop the trunk open. She then went to the quilt and started to pull it along the floor. Fortunately, the quilt made it much easier than she had expected to pull the body.

At the door, she had to wait for a couple to cross the parking lot and get into their car. Once they were pulling out, Danielle worked fast. She pulled the quilted body through the doorway and onto the porch. She took *some* care to not strike her father's head on the steps as she went down to the sidewalk, but not much.

There was a moment when she thought she would be caught—when a man came out of a townhouse just on the other side of the row. He turned to the right instantly, his back to them, as he headed for his car. His parked car was less than twenty-five yards away from where Danielle dragged her father's body in the quilt, but the darkness and the other parked cars blocked her perfectly. Besides, the man was in far too much of a hurry to even look her way.

Still, Danielle waited until he was out to keep moving. With that spike of fear in her heart, she moved faster. If anyone did happen to see her, it would be apparent that she was up to no good. But she put all of her energy and strength in dragging the quilt to the trunk of her car, dragging it so hard that the strand of duct tape around the legs started to come undone.

When she had the wrapped shape of her father by her trunk, she propped it up into a sitting position. Her shoulders were already sore, but she managed to find one more burst of strength to finish the job. Once again, as she wrapped her arms around his chest, she heard him groaning from under the quilt.

This did not make her afraid; if anything, it just pissed her off. She lifted as well as she could trying to use her legs for the bulk of her strength, and managed to wrestle him into the trunk. As she shifted his legs, bending them so he'd fit, a car swung into the parking lot, its headlights pointed in her direction. Instead of freezing, she went on with positioning the body, as if she was doing nothing more than loading up an old quilt.

He grumbled incoherently one more time. Danielle wished she still had the tea kettle. She slammed the trunk shut just as the car that had just pulled in coasted into a parking spot several spaces down. The driver was talking on his cell phone, totally oblivious to anything Danielle was doing.

Danielle slid in behind the wheel and pulled out of the lot, not quite sure where she was headed next. All she knew was that she had done more in the past ten minutes than she and Chloe together had done ever since their miserable father had been released from jail.

Danielle would handle this herself. She was sure Chloe would blow a gasket over how she had chosen to approach things, but Danielle honestly didn't care. She'd stopped caring about a lot of things over the last week or so and her sorry excuse for a father was one of them. Slowly, how her sister felt about her was closing in as a close second.

CHAPTER TWENTY FIVE

The company Mark Fairchild worked for was called Edgebrook Financial. As Chloe expected, the building was mostly dark when she and Rhodes walked through the front doors and into the lobby at 9:35. The only person in the lobby was a bored-looking security guard sitting behind the front desk. When he saw Chloe and Rhodes enter, he stood up and offered a smile.

"Can I help you ladies?" he asked.

They both pulled their IDs at the same times and it was Rhodes who ran through the introductions. "Rhodes and Fine, FBI," she said. "We're doing some follow-up work on a case that involves an employee of Edgebrook. We're coordinating with local PD if you have any questions."

The guard looked at the badges and nodded his approval. "What floor?" he asked.

It was information they had gleaned from the police reports, from the primary search of Mark's office. "Fourth floor," Chloe said.

"Got it. Elevators are down the hall. The fourth floor is totally empty tonight, so I'll shut the security system off. Don't want that thing bugging out for no reason."

"Thanks," Chloe said as she and Rhodes stepped away from the front desk and headed down the hallway toward the elevators.

On the fourth floor, they found the primary hallway dark and quiet. The hallway was illuminated by soft fluorescent lights and a single overhead that sat over what looked like a small receptionist's area. At the end of the hall was a large office, the door closed. The large glass pane in the door read **Mark Fairchild**. Chloe used the key Nolan had given them and they stepped into Mark's office without a problem.

Chloe flipped up the light switch on the wall alongside the door. The light revealed an office that was almost as large as Chloe's entire apartment. There was an enormous desk against the left wall, pushed almost to the back of the room. A small conference table sat in the center of the room with flat-screen TVs mounted on the wall to both sides.

"Any idea what we might be looking for?" Rhodes asked.

"No. Anything that looks like it doesn't belong. Hell, I'd be fine with Post-its with vague notes written on them."

The hard part of it was that Mark Fairchild seemed to keep a very clean office. Chloe figured this was the type of company that had a cleaning crew come in at least once a week to keep things looking tidy. As she approached his large desk, she noted that there wasn't a speck of dust anywhere in sight. All of his equipment—his monitor, keyboard, mouse, and pen holder, were all stainless steel or white.

She sat down behind the desk and looked around. There was an enormous whiteboard on the wall next to the desk. There were what seemed like hundreds of names, dates, locations, and assorted notes. While she looked around the desk, Rhodes took a picture of the whiteboard to catalogue the names and numbers.

Chloe opened up the top drawer on the desk. It was neatly organized, like everything else in the office. Pens, paperclips, a few USB sticks, and other assorted odds and ends. The right side of the desk contained three drawers along its support. She opened the first one and found only blank printer paper. She checked the second drawer and found assorted file folders, each one with a date on the top right; the most recent was from two years ago. The bottom drawer was empty. It was the largest of the drawers but looked to not have held anything in quite a while.

She closed it but then stopped. She thought she'd seen something just as she'd closed it. She opened the drawer back up and looked into the bottom. There was a crease running along the bottom of the drawer, situated a little less than halfway back. It looked as if someone had cut a thin grove into the bottom.

• "What is it?" Rhodes asked, coming over to look.

"A fake drawer, I think." She reached down and felt the groove. It was definitely part of the drawer's design. And when she pressed against the back end of the bottom, she felt it shift a bit. She then applied pressure to the other side of the drawer's bottom and heard a click. Still holding the smaller portion down, she wiggled her fingers into the groove and tried raising it, but nothing happened. She then tried sliding the smaller portion, and *that* worked. The false bottom slid back, feeding into another hidden compartment of the larger bottom drawer.

This revealed a space that was about six inches deep. Inside of it was a single USB drive, a cell phone, and what looked to be at first glance about a dozen bundles of one-hundred-dollar bills.

"Whoa," Rhodes said. "Jackpot, huh?"

Chloe nodded, thumbing through the stacks. There were actually sixteen stacks in all, each one containing fifty bills: eighty thousand dollars. But it wasn't the money that Chloe was truly interested in. Instead, she removed the USB and the phone. The phone was a burner, the sort you could buy with prepaid minutes at any convenience or drug store.

"Doesn't seem like the kind of phone a millionaire would keep around, does it?" Chloe asked.

"Nope," Rhodes agreed. "Makes me wonder what he uses it for."

"Let's just see."

Chloe powered the phone up and waited for it to load. When it did, she wasted no time navigating to the contacts and scrolling through them. There were no names assigned to the numbers, which made their job harder but also threw up more red flags. There were five numbers in all, called over and over again.

"Let me see if I can get Garcia on the phone," Rhodes said. "Maybe he can hook us up with someone to run these numbers."

Chloe nodded, feeling that the involvement of the assistant director made the case feel as if it was actually getting somewhere.

It took everything in her to not just go ahead and try calling the numbers; she knew that if she did, it could potentially clue Mark to the fact that he was being thoroughly investigated.

She listened as Rhodes spoke to Garcia. She was placed on hold and then started looking elsewhere around the office—at the built-in-bookshelves, at the pretentious abstract city-scape painting on the far wall. After a few minutes, she started talking again. When she did, she placed her cell phone on speaker and set it on the edge of Mark Fairchild's desk.

"Kim Moxley, you're on speaker with me and Agent Chloe Fine. Chloe will be giving you five phone numbers and we need them run down as quickly as possible."

"Can do," said a confident female voice on the other end. "Any idea if any of them are international?"

"Looks like at least one is," Chloe said.

"That one might take a bit longer. But I should be able to get you results for each of the other numbers within just a handful of seconds."

"Perfect," Chloe said. She then recited the first number. She was pretty sure the area code was one for New York and quickly found that she was correct.

"That one is to a man named Julio Alejos. It's a New York number, somewhere around Buffalo."

"How about this one?" Chloe asked, giving the second number.

After about ten seconds, Kim Moxley's voice responded. "That's a Boston number. A business called Polson and O'Neal Investments."

Chloe typed the names down as Moxley gave them. When she had down the name of the business, she went on with the numbers. The third turned out to be an unknown number that Moxley was unable to trace. "Not to worry, though," she said. "I'll work on it after this call and should be able to get results within a few hours."

Chloe then gave the fourth and fifth numbers. The results that came back were more than enough to make her feel that there was certainly some form of foul play going on. Even if it was not directly related to the murder of Jessie Fairchild, it seemed like Mark Fairchild was certainly up to something.

The fourth number was the international number, and Moxley, as she had warned, took a bit longer to get results. Still it took no more than thirty seconds before she was back with an answer. "What I can tell you for certain is that it's some offshore banking company. But there are two listings here, one under UXB Banking and another under West Bore Banking. Now, I ran the fifth number while waiting for that and it looks like that one is to a place called Collins Holdings."

"A holdings company and an offshore bank connection," Rhodes said.

"Seems that way," Moxley said. "Hopefully, I'll have that unknown number cracked for you within a few hours."

"Thanks for your help," Rhodes said. "Please keep us posted if you discover anything else."

She killed the call and pocketed her cell phone. "Things just started to look pretty bad for Mark Fairchild," she said. "Even if those calls had been made from his personal phone and not a hidden cell, it would raise questions."

"It makes me wonder what is on this USB," Chloe said. She fired up the monitor and placed the USB into the small port located to the side of the monitor. She was fully expecting it to be password protected but there was nothing of the sort. The file folder popped up and she was able to open it without a problem.

There was a video file on the stick. She hovered over the thumbnail and saw that it was simply named MOVIE. It was forty-three minutes long. She opened it up and knew what it was within the first ten seconds. There was a woman on a large bed. She was totally naked with the exception of a pair of thongs that were so thin they may as well not have been there at all. There was a huge painting over an ornate headboard, giving them enough video to show that this had not been filmed in the Fairchild home. Chloe would have snapped out of the video then and there but she wanted to make sure the woman was not Jessie Fairchild. It was impossible to tell from the splayed form of the body, the legs parted and slightly raised.

When Mark Fairchild entered the shot from the left, he wore only a pair of boxer shorts. When the woman on the bed leaned over, grabbed them and started yanking them down seductively, Chloe could finally see the woman's face. It was most definitely not Jessie.

"I wonder if it's one of those expensive escorts," Rhodes commented.

Chloe stopped the video and took out the USB. She had no intention of finding out *who* the woman was. Idly, she wondered if the huge amount of cash in the hidden drawer was to pay for those escorts.

"I've seen enough," Chloe said. "You good here, Rhodes?"

"Yeah. I think we've got enough. Nothing left to do but wait for the bigger cogs in DC to do their thing."

They left Mark's office, closing and locking the door behind them. They made their way back down the dimly lit hallway and as they reached the elevators, Chloe couldn't help but feel that the case was coming to a close. Surely the suspicious phone numbers would lead to something. And she was growing more and more certain that *something* would be the revelation that Mark Fairchild killed his wife.

Chapter Twenty Six

When Chloe arrived in her apartment at 11:17 that night, she stood in the doorway for a moment and looked at the remaining mess left over from Danielle's break-in. She had fully intended to call her sister today but the case had started to move a bit and she'd simply forgotten. She considered calling anyway, despite the late hour, but figured it could wait. Besides…she'd see Danielle soon enough; she fully intended to take her up on her offer to clean the place up.

She walked into the apartment and didn't even bother pretending she was going to do anything other than grab a quick shower and go to bed. She didn't go by the fridge for a snack or a glass of wine, nor did she even think about turning on the television. She started stripping down before she even reached her bedroom and was shower-ready before turning on the water.

As she soaked, she again wondered how she could have let her own emotional hell so easily blind her to the facts of the case. More than that, if her feelings toward her father had changed so drastically, why was she still leaning toward sympathy with men like Mark Fairchild when all clues pointed to his guilt?

Maybe she'd end up taking Dr. Fischer up on another session after all. If she was going to truly move on from her past, vulnerability and therapy were things she was going to have to strongly consider.

She got out, dried off, and was in bed by midnight. It didn't take her long to fall asleep, but when she did, she found her thoughts turning toward a smaller part of the case—a part that had nearly gone overlooked: the ring that had been used to gruesomely tear into Jessie Fairchild's neck.

She still couldn't help but feel that someone was making some sort of statement, but she wasn't sure what that statement was.

It was the last thread that wound through her head as she drifted off to sleep.

Later, she was stirred awake, not by the alarm on her phone, but the sound of it ringing. She slapped at the bedside table for it while glaring at the clock. She winced when she saw that it was only 4:48 in the morning. She picked up the phone, clicked on her bedside lamp, and saw Rhodes's name and number on the call display.

"Rhodes. It's early. I hope this means there's news."

"There is. Kim Moxley was true to her word and called when there was news. And holy shit, is there news."

"Where are you?"

"On the way to your apartment. How soon can you get ready?"

"Very fast. Fill me in, would you?"

Chloe put the phone on speaker and got out of bed, suddenly very much awake.

"Well, the unknown number ended up being tacked on a guy that had been accused of criminal financial practices a few years back, but he got off clean. Mitchell Beck. That name ring a bell by any chance?"

"None."

"It meant nothing to me, either. Anyway, Beck used to work for one of those places that deals in hedge funds. A few brains at headquarters put the filter of Beck's old case over what we've got going on with Mark Fairchild and it all looked very similar. So they did some digging and after just a few calls and a quick visit by a field agent in our New York office, we're now pretty much able to confirm that Mark was laundering money from Collins Holdings into a hedge fund that he had set up in secret some time ago. And Mitchell Beck was at the center of it all."

"So that's more than enough to arrest." She was slipping into a pair of pants now. All she had left to do was make sure her hair wasn't a hot mess before heading out the door.

"It is... but it gets better. The name Julio Alejos—the name Moxley got for us last night—is also closely tied to our criminal friend Mitchell Beck. He's been on the watch list up in New York for the last three or four years under suspicion of being the heart and soul of a major drug cartel. The New York field agent and some boys from the NYPD paid him a visit about two hours ago. To save his own ass, he started naming names. Most of it was dealing with the drug cartel, so he was surprised when the agent mentioned Mark Fairchild's name. He confirmed that he had been in talks with Mark Fairchild recently, but would not say why they were speaking. Because of that, he's currently being held in custody."

"This is all red-handed type stuff," Chloe said as she holstered her Glock and strapped the holster onto her belt. "But what the hell does it have to do with Jessie's death?"

"That picture still isn't clear. But we've got money laundering and involvement with a man who's highly suspected of being the center of a huge drug cartel. Adding murder of a spouse in there doesn't seem too far of a stretch."

"Not a stretch at all," Chloe agreed.

"Now... I'm about a block away from your place. You ready to go pay Mark a visit?"

They'd called ahead to the Falls Church PD as a courtesy and for request with an assist. So when Chloe drove into the main stretch of Mark Fairchild's neighborhood, she wasn't surprised by the sight of the two patrol cars parked at the end of Mark's block. It was 5:37 when she pulled their car into the Fairchilds' driveway, a little less than fifty minutes after Rhodes had woken her up with the call.

There were no flashing lights, no sirens. As Chloe and Rhodes stepped out of their car, Deputy Nolan pulled in behind them. The three of them were as quiet as possible as they gathered together in front of the Fairchild steps—the very same steps Mark had stood on top of to let the media know that he planned to donate all of the money from his wife's life insurance policy. They gave one another a brief glance, making sure everyone was ready to roll in. Chloe took the lead, with Rhodes behind her and Nolan bringing up the rear.

Chloe knocked on the door. It sounded loud in the otherwise quiet of the neighborhood. She assumed that pretty close to now all of the younger, fit types would be spotted on the sidewalks, getting in their morning runs. Others would be walking their dogs. But for now, just as the sun started to tease them with dawn, the neighborhood was absolutely silent and still.

When there was no answer after thirty seconds, Chloe knocked again. This time, a few seconds after the knock, a light came on in the house. She could just barely see the glow of it through the window several feet away from the door. A few seconds later, they heard shuffling footsteps approaching the door.

"Who's there?" Mark Fairchild asked from the other side of the door.

"It's Agents Fine and Rhodes," Chloe said. "Deputy Nolan is with us, too."

The sound of the door unlocking could be heard at once. Mark didn't bother with just cracking the door to peer out; he opened it all the way. He was looking at them with muted hope. He was still struggling to come fully awake, but he seemed almost happy to see them.

"Did you find something?" he asked.

"We did," Chloe said. "Mr. Fairchild, can we come in?"

He hesitated here but nodded slowly. He stepped to the side and let the two agents and Deputy Nolan into his home. He led them into the living room, where Chloe saw evidence that he had been sleeping on the couch. A pillow and two scattered blankets were on the couch, his cell phone sitting on the coffee table.

Mark saw her checking the couch out and chuckled nervously. "I can't bring myself to go into the bedroom yet...let alone sleep in it."

Chloe ignored this pity play and went straight to the point of the matter. "Mr. Fairchild, we found your burner phone. Bottom drawer of your office desk, in that little cut-away compartment."

Mark's face went absolutely blank at this comment. He looked at each of them, one after the other as if his neck was on a timed spring. "That's...that's trespassing. That phone is company property and—"

"Why hide company property?" Rhodes asked.

"Was the hidden USB with the video on it company property as well?" Chloe asked.

At this, Mark looked like she had reached out and slapped him. His face was taking on a huge range of emotions. It was a look Chloe had seen hundreds of times before—the look of a man who was watching his elaborate story crumble...his entire world shaking under his feet. His mouth opened as if he had something to say, but no words came out.

"Julio Alejos has confirmed that he knows you and has been speaking with you," Chloe said. "That alone is bad enough but just tonight, the FBI discovered a link between Alejos and a man named Mitchell Beck. But I feel like you already know about that link because they've somehow had a hand in your money laundering, haven't they?"

"Julio was a mistake," he said. "I know that now. I know...shit." He sat down hard on the couch. His hands were trembling and he suddenly seemed to find the floor very interesting.

"How does it all tie to Jessie?" Rhodes asked.

Mark looked up at them again, shaking his head. "I swear to you. I swear to you on my life that I did not kill my wife."

"Discoveries we've made in the past several hours make me not so prone to believe you," Chloe said.

"People saw me at work. I have alibis. I can't be two places at once!"

"Then who did you hire?" Chloe asked. "Was it Alejos? Maybe one of his people?"

"No! With all due respect, you're fucking crazy if you think I killed my wife. The whole reason I was doing this shit…this laundering and working with Julio Alejos…it was to make sure we were taken care of. I had pissed away so much money, and Jessie was so used to spending it. I had to make sure we were covered. I wanted the best for her so why the hell would I kill her?"

He was nearly screaming when he came to the end of it. Tears ran down his face and now when he looked at them, he looked more like a kid who had gotten in trouble with some bad kids at school and was waiting for someone to forgive him for his deeds or to bail him out.

"When you initially spoke with Beck at Collins Holding, did you know they were a front? Did you know from the start that the company was a front for the cartel that Julio Alejos is thought to be the leader of?"

"Yes."

"How did you get that information?" Nolan asked.

"I can't say. It's too dangerous. I can't…"

"Julio Alejos has already started naming people just to save his own skin," Rhodes said. "The last I heard about an hour ago, four arrests have already been made. People like that…there's not much honesty or loyalty among them."

"There are too many people involved," Mark said. "I can't risk it."

"It really doesn't matter," Chloe said. She reached under her jacket and withdrew her cuffs. When Mark saw them, he only frowned. He had resigned himself to this in the few moments between the first mention of Julio Alejos and Mitchell Beck and now.

"I don't know what happened," he said. "I didn't kill her. I swear it."

"All the same," Chloe said. "Mark Fairchild, you're under arrest for money laundering, investment fraud, possibly life insurance conspiracy, and speculation of, at the very least, serving as an accomplice in the murder of your wife."

Mark shook his head the whole time, but he stood up and allowed easy access to his wrists. He did not fight when she cuffed him, nor when she led him out of the house. The only thing he said was to Deputy Nolan as he passed by on the porch, on the way to the cars below.

"I suggest you and the entire PD lawyer the fuck up. I intend to make this entire thing hell for you."

CHAPTER TWENTY SEVEN

Chloe and Rhodes sat at the conference room table in the back of the Falls Church PD, sipping coffee and staying updated on the events following the arrest of Mark Fairchild. The updates came in the form of phone calls from Kim Moxley and the small team that had connected the dots the night before. They also came from visits from Nolan, coming by the room while he fielded calls from media, lawyers, and partners with the state police.

So far, the only real news was that every single bit of Mark's assets had been seized within three hours of his arrest. His bank accounts had been frozen, Jessie's life insurance policy had been temporarily suspended, and the hedge fund that he had been trying to hide was being dissolved. Whether or not he knew any of this, Chloe did not know; as far as she knew, Mark was being prepped for a trip to DC. She wasn't sure if he'd ride along with her and Rhodes or not. No, he'd be escorted in a black sedan with tinted windows and interrogated for days about his involvement with Julio Alejos and Mitchell Beck.

Chloe was on her second cup of coffee when the uneasiness in her stomach became something more akin to a hunch. She'd felt an inkling of it the day before when she and Rhodes had argued about Mark's guilt. It was back now, almost in an *I-told-you-so* sort of way.

"You look troubled," Rhodes said from her side of the table.

"I am. Yeah, we nailed Mark Fairchild on a variety of financial crimes and might have even been able to use his money laundering scheme to expose Beck and Alejos, but it still doesn't tie him to his wife's murder."

"There are so many shady characters involved in this thing now that the list of potential killers is almost *too* long, though," Rhodes said.

"You think Mark hired someone?" Chloe asked.

"I don't know. If those tears and frustration he showed last night were fake, the man is a *damned* good actor. I think he was ... I don't know ..."

"Scared. I think that's the word you're looking for."

Rhodes nodded right at the same time Chloe's phone started to ring. She saw Johnson's name in the ID screen and answered it right away.

"You and Rhodes have started a pretty big domino effect," Johnsons said, skipping a greeting entirely. "At this very moment, one Julio Alejos is being transported to Washington, DC, on a string of charges related to the financial mess Mark Fairchild was involved in. We've been trying to nail him on *anything* for the last three years and this case you guys cracked is the cause of it."

"But the case isn't cracked," Chloe said. "We still don't have an ID on Jessie Fairchild's killer."

"Not yet. But I guarantee you it will come up in these interrogations. Probably not Alejos—he's too seasoned. But probably one of the guys he's rolling over on. Trust me, Chloe. I've seen this kind of thing before. The case, as far as you and Rhodes are concerned, is about as closed as it's going to get. Someone will either fess up or rat someone else out before too long."

"All the same, I'd like to stay on the case for another day or so."

"On what grounds?"

"Well, we found the phone that led to this so-called domino effect in his office—a place he spent most of his time. I'd like to go back and speak to some of his co-workers."

"The local PD down there already did that."

"Yes sir. But I haven't."

She heard Johnson stifling a laugh. He appreciated a bit of cockiness but never came out and said such. "If you must, Fine. One more day. That's it. I'd actually like you and Rhodes down here to question Julio Alejos. Maybe *you* can be the one to get something out of him. You might be able to find out who the killer is from a man that was in New York when it happened."

"Any idea when he's due at headquarters?"

"Looking at around two or so this afternoon, I think."

"We'll see you then."

She ended the call and found Rhodes looking at her. She sipped from her coffee thoughtfully. "Did you just turn down an invite to come in for the day and call this case closed?"

"I did. I'm sorry. But the more I think about it … someone had to have sensed something those last few days before she was killed. Maybe someone at Mark's office noticed him being *off* somehow."

"It feels like a stretch to me."

"It might be. But we came here to solve a murder and I'd really like to make sure that's done … or, at least, make sure I've done my very best."

"Yeah, yeah, let's go then," Rhodes said.

She was clearly not a fan of the idea but was already getting to her feet. It wasn't nearly as bad as yesterday's irritation, which Chloe considered a win. Slowly, they were starting to learn to work well together. And as this case came to an end that might turn out to be nothing more than one big question mark, they were both starting to feel the incomplete nature of it.

Apparently, being so close to a sense of failure really brought partners together.

Edgebrook Financial looked like a totally different building in the light of day with its parking lot nearly filled to capacity. When they entered the building, even the lobby looked completely different, Natural light flooded the area, spilling in from large glass panes over the doors, each pane standing about twenty feet tall. People were filing in and out of the lobby, out of doors, down hallways, and into elevators.

The guard behind the front desk area was a different one from the night before. Being business hours, they didn't stop by the desk but ventured deeper into the lobby and headed to the elevators again. When they arrived on the fourth floor, it was more of the same from the lobby; a hallway that had been darkened and dead the night before was suddenly alive with activity.

They stopped by the receptionist's area they had passed by the night before. A beautiful twenty-something woman sat behind the desk, looking like she had been specifically crafted for the job.

"Hello there, ladies," the receptionist said in a rehearsed tone. "Can I help you?"

Chloe subtly flashed her ID, not wanting to cause a stir. "I'm Agent Fine, with the FBI. I was hoping I could speak to someone who had worked closely with Mark Fairchild sometime during the last several weeks."

"Oh, okay," she said. "Is everything okay? We noticed he hadn't come in today. He tried for a few days but we figured he still hadn't quite healed."

"I honestly can't discuss it," Chloe said. "Does anyone come to mind?"

"Certainly. If you head down the hall and stop at the second door on the right, that's Jason Earhart's office. They were working on a finding project for some sort of nuclear decommissioning project up until Jessie was killed."

"Was there a working relationship before that?"

"Yes. The police have spoken to him already. Jason and Mark were sort of the perfect tag-team. Whenever there was a big job to knock out, they were the ones to nail it down."

"Thanks," Chloe said a she turned away and headed to the right.

"You recall Jason Earhart's name from any of the reports?" Rhodes asked.

"No. But I do think I heard the name in passing within the department—maybe between Nolan and Clifton. I'm not sure."

They came to Earhart's door and knocked, though it was half-way open. A tired but loud response came at once: "Yeah, it's open!"

Chloe and Rhodes stepped in. The office they stepped into was roughly the same size as Mark's, though not quite as tidy. His desk was also much more basic—presumably because he did not need hideaway drawers. The man sitting behind the desk looked to be a little younger than Mark. He was slightly heavyset and wore his hair in a style that made it apparent he cared nothing for the way he looked at the office. It hung down across his brow, nearly touching his eyebrows.

"Can I help you?" he asked.

Chloe stepped forward, showing her ID. As she did, Rhodes nonchalantly closed the door behind them.

"We need to ask you some questions about Mark Fairchild."

"The police have already asked me a ton," he said. He did not sound irritated, though. If anything, he sounded bored.

"Have you, by chance, gotten a call from him today? Or maybe even *about* him?"

"No. Why? Is something wrong?"

"It will be public knowledge soon enough, so there's no harm in letting you know. But as of about three hours ago, Mark is in some very bad trouble. He's been placed under arrest for various counts of financial fraud and possible involvement in the murder of his wife."

Earhart looked legitimately confused, almost comically so. He then let out a nervous laugh and shook his head. "With all due respect, I call bullshit. There's no way. That's just not the sort of man Mark is."

"We've got a stream of growing evidence that says it is," Rhodes said.

"He's also confirmed some of it to us with his own mouth," Chloe added.

Earhart was visibly shaken. He leaned back in his chair, his face going pale. He swept some of the hair off of his brow, making him look much older somehow.

"Mr. Earhart, I need you to think hard about something. I want you to think about Mark's demeanor over the last few weeks. Was there anything at all about the way he acted or even in the way he carried himself here at work that you found the least bit strange? I don't care how small it might have seemed. I need to know anything you can think of."

Earhart sighed, sat forward, and placed his elbows on his desk. He looked like a child sitting at attention. When he spoke, Chloe thought he might start crying.

"Mark was never really one to close his door. He was all about being available. He'd close it if he was in an important meeting or on a heated phone call, but that's about it. These last few weeks, though…it seemed like he had it shut more often than usual. I never even consider it as odd until just now…when you asked the question."

"He was here in the morning Jessie was killed, right?" Rhodes asked.

"He was."

"Anything out of the ordinary that morning?"

"Not really. It was a Friday, so there was an all-hands meeting—but he showed up late. Again, no big deal. A few people straggle in late for those meetings. But not Mark. He was usually among the first. He always joked he got to those meetings early to snag the best donuts."

"Did you speak to him at all that morning?"

"Yeah, about this project he and I had been working on. And you know…"

He trailed off here, his eyes wandering as he collected his thoughts.

"What is it, Mr. Earhart?"

"He did seem sort of distracted. I had to sort of rein him in a few times. He was forgetting names and figures—which he rarely does. Again, it was nothing huge. I work closely with him a lot. Anyone else would have probably not even noticed."

"Can you recall what you were doing when he got the call from the police?" Chloe asked.

"Well, I didn't even know about it until about fifteen minutes later. I was on a call and Kaitlin, the receptionist, knocked on my door. I sternly shooed her away because the call I was on was a very important one. When I was off of the call, I went out to see what she wanted. Most of the entire floor was sort of morose, very quiet. Kaitlin told me that the police had called, looking for Mark. They told him over the phone that his wife had been killed. From what I understand, there was a police escort downstairs for him."

"Do you know if he spoke to anyone after receiving the call?"

"I asked around—as did the police—but apparently, Kaitlin was the only one. And she said he was sort of *blank*. Processing it, you know? He told her in an almost dry fashion: *My wife is dead,* and headed for the elevators. Someone down in the lobby—a guy that works on the second floor, said when Mark got off of the elevators, he hit his knees and started wailing. The police escort helped him out of the building and then he was gone."

"And that's all you know?"

"It is. I just … I just have to say that if Mark *did* have something to do with his wife's murder, I would be absolutely shocked."

"And the financial stuff?" Rhodes asked.

"I'd be shocked, but it might be easier to convince me. Mark liked making money. He liked taking care of his wife. He'd brag all of the time about being able to spoil her."

Chloe and Rhodes exchanged a look of frustration. Nothing new had come out of this, other than finding out that Mark liked to spoil Jessie—which they'd already surmised. Still, the idea that Mark had seemed nervous and distracted the morning of his wife's death … did that mean he'd *known* it was going to happen? Were all of those closed-door calls he made related to her eventual murder?

These were questions that were not going to be answered by Jason Earhart or anyone else in the Edgebrook offices. If there were any answers to be had, they'd come from interrogation rooms back in DC later this afternoon.

"Thank you very much for your time, Mr. Earhart," Chloe said.

He nodded and looked as if he wanted to say something else but kept quiet in the end. "Of course," he said. "Let me know if there is anything else I can do."

Chloe and Rhodes walked out of the office and back down the hallway. In the elevator, Chloe leaned back against the wall and tilted her head up with a sigh. "The more information we have, the less this is making sense," she said.

"I can't help but wonder if Mark pissed someone off," Rhodes said. "If his wife's murder was some sort of retaliation."

"I thought that, too. But he came to work that day. And even with all of this financial trouble going on the background, he was willingly giving over information. It just makes zero sense to me."

"The loose ends will get tied up this afternoon," Rhodes said. There was hope in her voice, but not much. Chloe could tell this was started to take its toll on her as well.

"Let's just do what Johnson suggested," Chloe said. "Get back to DC and wait for Alejos to show up. Maybe they'll have some more info on Mitchell Beck by then."

"Feels like too many threads. Too many ways to get sidetracked."

"Or all those threads will tie up into one neat little bow," Chloe pointed out.

Rhodes chuckled. "You've sort of done a one-eighty on me since yesterday. Anything you want to share?"

Chloe smiled and said, "Maybe one day. For now, though, let's keep my skeletons in their closet and go dig up Mark Fairchild's."

CHAPTER TWENTY EIGHT

Director Johnson looked like he had been running a marathon when Chloe and Rhodes stepped into his office at 11:45 that morning. He looked worn out and quite excited, especially when he sat down behind his desk mere moments after Chloe and Rhodes took the two seats on the opposite side of the desk. He took a moment to sink into his chair and then leaned forward with a weary smile on his face.

"This thing is moving faster than we expected," he said. "First of all, good job on getting the ball rolling. I know it might have been an accidental discovery, but this little discovery has also inadvertently given us enough intel to finally get Julio Alejos into custody."

"So where are we now?"

"The latest update—and it could be different by now because things are coming in so quickly—is that Julio Alejos was absolutely talking to Mark Fairchild. We still aren't quite sure why. We also know that Mitchell Beck was speaking with Fairchild, but there isn't quite enough evidence. There are a lot of dead ends there and I honestly don't even know if we'll have enough to pin Beck down. It's been tried before but the man is like a magician when it comes to lawyers and loopholes."

"And we're happy to help with those threads any way we can," Chloe said. "But at the end of the day, I'm still looking for Jessie Fairchild's killer."

"I understand that," Johnson said. "It's one of many layers to this onion. And I've already talked it over with the team that was responsible for apprehending Alejos and bringing him in. You two have first dibs on him when he gets here. As bad as it sounds, the murder of Jessie Fairchild is on the lower end of the potential things we can pin on Alejos and his drug cartel."

"So what can we do now?" Rhodes asked. "I can't bear to just sit around and wait."

"And you won't have to," he said. He slid a sheet of paper over to them, moving quickly and with purpose even in something so simple. "Here are call records from a burner phone we found in Alejos's house. It's been deactivated for about three days. There was another one, but he destroyed it before we could get him into custody."

Rhodes took the paper and Chloe looked at it as they scanned it together. There were about thirty calls in all, most made to the same few numbers over and over again.

"Have these been checked yet?" Chloe asked.

"No. We just got this list together about half an hour ago and I wanted the two of you on it. We do already know that one of the numbers on there is a direct line to Mark Fairchild's office."

"I'll get on this right now," Rhodes said. "We worked with a woman named Kim Moxley on the numbers we found in Mark's office. Can I use her as a resource?"

"Please do. There's a big stirring of excitement around here. Use anything and anyone you need. If we can bring this guy down, it will unravel one of the biggest drug cartels on the East Coast."

"In other words, no pressure, right?" Chloe said.

It garnered a laugh from Johnson, but there was very little joy behind it.

For the next hour and a half, Chloe and Rhodes sat in a small basement office with Kim Moxley. Moxley was, for lack of a better word, interesting. She had short cropped hair that had been dyed raven black, the blonde roots unapologetically showing. She was a rail-thin specimen of a woman but though she was small in stature, she was enormous in personality. Her voice was loud and her laugh was even louder. Chloe decided she liked the woman right away. In a strange way, she reminded her a bit of Danielle.

She was doing little more than entering each of the numbers from Julio Alejos's burner phone into a piece of software that Chloe was not familiar with. Apparently, because the phone had been deactivated, it was a bit harder to connect the numbers and the calls with the phone. She had to make a few calls to verify the authenticity of the phone, right down to which Walgreens in Albany, New York, it had been purchased from.

They were not at all surprised to see that two of the numbers were exactly the same as numbers that had been pulled from Mark Fairchild's phone: the one to the offshore bank and the unknown and unlisted one that had been pinned to Mitchell Beck. The others were to a man that was listed in the FBI database as Julio's brother and then a personal line to a man named Luca Valenz. Valenz was one of the names Julio had offered up and was currently being held in a holding cell in upstate New York. A known drug dealer and convicted rapist, he had enough of a record for any involvement with a drug cartel to put him away for a very long time.

The last number they inserted into the software turned out to be another unlisted number. The three women seemed to sigh all together, coming to this roadblock.

"How long did it take to pin the other unlisted number to Beck?" Chloe asked.

"About three hours."

"Same for this one?"

"Probably. Though we can apply some of the things we learned last night and maybe get some clues while we're waiting."

"How's that?" Chloe asked.

"The number he called might be an unlisted one, but we can find out where the phone was located when Alejos called it."

"Yeah, that *could* help," Chloe said.

"It'd be a long shot," Rhodes agreed. "But yeah, we may as well give it a go."

"One second," Moxley said. She inputted something into her system and slurped down what seemed like half of a mug of coffee while she waited. "Results are coming in," she said several seconds later. "He called the number seven times within the last month. Four times, the recipient phone was located in New York. A fifth and sixth, it was in Boston."

New York, Chloe thought. *Makes sense, because that's Alejos's stomping grounds. Boston... can't be a coincidence that's where the Fairchilds moved from. If the next listing is...*

"Seventh call came from New York City, and the recipient phone was in Falls Church, Virginia."

"Got a date on that?" Chloe asked, a chill riding sharply down her spine.

"Hold one sec," Moxley said, the excitement also apparent in her voice. She then smiled and gave them a smile and a nod. "Holy shit. The call to Falls Church was made last Friday at nine-oh-five."

Chloe got to her feet. She had nowhere to go at the moment, but the realization tis brought to her would not let her sit still.

"That's got to be the killer. We have to find out who that unlisted number is."

"I'll push it to the top of the priorities pile," Moxley said.

Chloe's phone buzzed in her pocket. When she saw that it was Johnson, she sensed that this was it. This was the call that was going to push them toward the end of the case. Selfishly, she only hoped it would be an ending that actually *felt* like an ending. Despite the huge revelations with Alejos, Beck, and Fairchild, Chloe could not help but feel that she owed it to Jessie Fairchild to find her killer.

"This is Fine," she answered.

"Head up to Interrogation Room Three," Johnson said. "Alejos is here."

Director Johnson, Assistant Director Garcia, and two agents Chloe had never met were standing outside of Interrogation Room Three.

She assumed the other two agents were the men from New York who had taken Alejos in. As she and Rhodes approached, all four men looked in their direction.

"Agent Fine, Agent Rhodes, this is Agent Keller and Agent Labitski out of New York. You can thank them for bringing out guest right to our front door."

"And as far as I'm concerned, you can keep him," the one named Keller said. "He's quiet, but he's an ass about it. He's bad news. I know it sounds cliché, and I'm sorry."

"Anything we need to watch out for?" Rhodes asked.

"He gets under your skin. The ride down here was a long one. Two times, I thought I was going to pull over and shoot him in the head."

"Did he say anything that might point towards his guilt?"

"No," Labitski said. "Not in the money laundering stuff or a murder."

"I will let you know that he said he was looking forward to see what corrupted DC agent would be sent in to handle him," Keller said.

"Then let's show him," Chloe said. She looked at Johnson and asked: "May we?"

"Yes. But listen … you heard Keller. This guy will try to rile you up, to piss you off. If either of you feel yourselves losing your cool, you step out. Understood?"

Both women nodded as Chloe started for the door. When she opened it, she felt a brief spike of nervousness. She was about to interrogate perhaps the nastiest man she had ever met—certainly the nastiest she had ever interrogated. And knowing that her case was at the lower end of the man's totem pole made her all the more aware that she might not be the right person for this interrogation.

But when she closed the door after Rhodes entered, the sound of the door closing calmed her. It also helped that the man sitting behind the small steel interrogation table looked perfectly normal. He was Hispanic, probably in his mid-thirties, and was dressed in a plain gray T-shirt and dark jeans. His hair was close-cropped and if he didn't look so smug, he might have come off as handsome.

"Really?" Alejos said. "This is what I get? Two women? Damn, if this city isn't trying to insert a woman into *everything*!" He chuckled at his own joke and shook his head.

"Do you have something against women?" Chloe asked.

"Not at all. I love women. Maybe too much. But if you're here to try to make me speak, this is a job where you should never send a woman to do a man's job."

"Thanks for the consideration, but I think we'll do fine," Chloe said. "Besides ... if I'm going to be honest with you, I should let you know something. It might surprise you, but I think we should start out with honesty. You okay with that?"

"You can be as honest as you want. I can promise no such thing."

"Well, here goes: I don't care why the FBI is currently on your ass. You're not that big of a deal to me. They think you run some big drug cartel in New York. I don't care. Doesn't take much skill to sell drugs in NYC, does it?"

Alejos grinned at her. He rolled his eyes and sat back in his chair. "If you're trying this passive reverse psychology nonsense, it won't work with me."

"Oh, it's not reverse psychology. Like I said ... I'm all about honesty here. Agent Rhodes and I don't give two shits about whatever you're peddling up north. She and I were assigned to a case in Falls Church several days ago. A case where we got to meet a man named Mark Fairchild face to face. That name ring a bell for you?"

"Rings a big bell. That man is very stupid. He was promising at first but he got away from himself."

"How do you mean?" Rhodes asked.

Alejos slowly sat up. Chloe saw the slightest sense of ease in his face. He was sliding into the exact frame of mind she wanted. He was relaxed, thinking this was another situation where he could throw someone else under the bus and be done with it.

"Let's just say he has a problem with money," Alejos said. "Let's say he crossed some of the wrong people."

"Were you one of those people?" Rhodes asked.

"Maybe."

"How about Mitchell Beck? Was he one of them, too?"

"I don't know anything about Beck. I don't know why you assholes keep insisting he and I are in bed together."

"But you know him?"

"Yes, I do. Unfortunately."

"Does Mark Fairchild know him?"

"Yeah. Beck called me to ask about him."

"What for?" Chloe asked.

"Wanted to know if knew who Fairchild was. If he'd ever worked with me before."

"Mr. Alejos, do you know what happened to Mark Fairchild last Friday?"

"The agents that took me in in New York said someone killed his wife. Said they hadn't found a killer yet." He paused here and then gave them an exasperated look. "You think I did it or something? That's ridiculous. I got at least fifty people that can prove I was in New York last Friday."

"I'm sure you do," Chloe said. "And I was suggesting no such thing. What I *would* like to know, though, is who you were calling in Falls Church on that very same Friday morning...a call that happened to be placed just before Mark Fairchild's wife happened to be killed."

The ease on his face evaporated and turned to anger. "You think you're a clever bitch, huh?"

"At times."

"Mr. Alejos, think about it," Rhodes said. "The bureau seized your phone—a burner phone that, let's face it, seems suspicious in the possession of a bigshot such as yourself. We got your phone records from that phone. We know all of the calls you made on it, so we *know* you made a call to Falls Church."

"And you've also admitted to knowing Mark Fairchild, who lives in Falls Church. Do the math. It's not looking good for you."

"If you say so."

Chloe smirked and nodded. "I don't get it. You've already thrown so many people under the bus today. Seems you have no problem with that. So why not just one more? Tell me who you were calling."

"Tell us," Rhodes said. "Just a name. Like Agent Fine said … we don't care anything about the drugs up in New York. We want to find the man that killed Jessie Fairchild."

Alejos just shook his head. "I'm not saying anything else to you."

"Seems unlike you from what I hear," Chloe said. She leaned in close to the table and smirked again. "Guess that means I stumped you, huh?"

She could see Alejos fighting to bite back a remark. There was anger in his eyes unlike any she had ever seen before.

"You may as well tell us," Chloe said. "Because of those phone records, you're going to be charged with being an accessory at least. If you can offer up the killer, maybe we can get that negated."

Alejos smiled politely at the agents and then showed him both of his middle fingers.

"Fine," Chloe said, headed for the door. "We're quite happy to take partial credit for being the ones that helped get you into prison."

Before Chloe and Rhodes could make their exit, Alejos let out a little barking laugh. "It's cute you think that way, little girl."

"Why's that?" Chloe hissed through her teeth without turning to face him.

"I'll be out in no time. Probably by tomorrow morning. Mark my words on that."

Somehow, Chloe let the words slide right off of her back as she stepped out the door. This time, when the door closed behind them, the sound irritated her and she could identify with Keller; while Alejos had really not been all that disrespectful or problematic, she had the sudden urge to put a bullet in the man's skull.

She and Rhodes walked into the neighboring room, a small observation room where a flat-screen on the wall showed the inside of the interrogation room. Johnson, Garcia, Keller, and Labitski sat in folding chairs, looking at the screen.

"I see what you mean," Chloe told Keller. "I'd really like to blow his brains out at this point."

"Hey, that was pretty good," Johnson said. "You backed him into a corner and he didn't even realize it. He basically admitted that he did in fact place a call to Falls Church on the morning Jessie Fairchild was killed."

"But without a name, we have nothing," Chloe said.

"There are a lot of moving pieces," Garcia said. "If we can get Mitchell Beck into a room and he knows that Julio Alejos is also in an interrogation room *and* that he's already given four names to save his own ass…I think that's our best bet."

"Any movement on his arrest?" Chloe asked.

"There's a quiet manhunt of sorts all over the state of New York," Keller said.

"Fine…Rhodes…go home," Johnson said. "Rest up and meet us back here in the morning."

"Sir, it's not even four o' clock," Chloe said.

"I know. But you two have been busting your ass. Take the afternoon and meet us back here tomorrow morning at eight. If any updates come in the meantime, you'll be among the first to know."

Chloe didn't even see the point in arguing. Based on what she was being told, all she could do was sit and wait for Mitchell Beck to be arrested. And she had already been told that his arrest might not even happen because he seemed to slide out of the grip of the law on a fairly continuous basis.

"Come on," Rhodes said, nudging her. "He's right. The case is getting to you. It's getting to me, too. Maybe you should get out of here before you *do* go back in there and do or say something you'll regret."

Chloe looked back up at the screen. The man sitting at that steel table was not Jessie Fairchild's killer, but she would bet anything that he knew who was. She would go even further and venture a bet that he had likely even assigned someone to commit the murder.

And he wouldn't budge. He'd gotten so used to getting his way and keeping two steps ahead of the police and the FBI that he felt he could get away with it. Yes... maybe it *was* best that she went home.

Besides... she had her own issues to wrestle with at home. She needed to call Danielle, to make sure she was okay after the talk the other night. And to have her come clean the rest of the mess in her apartment.

But as she walked out of the viewing room with Rhodes at her side, she looked back at the screen on the wall once more. She knew it was unlikely, but she could have sworn the bastard was smiling at her.

Chloe clenched her jaw and looked away. She decided then and there that she'd do whatever she could to get Julio Alejos behind bars, even if she *did* have to push the boundaries of professionalism.

CHAPTER TWENTY NINE

Chloe waited until she got home to call Danielle. During the drive, she allowed herself to calm down, to become less enraged by the absolute arrogance of Julio Alejos. It worked to some degree; when she arrived at her apartment, she no longer felt any homicidal urges toward the man. She put on a kettle for tea and made the call to Danielle.

The phone went directly to voicemail. Chloe rolled her eyes, assuming her sister had decided to take one of her random afternoon naps. She wondered if Danielle was even looking for a job anymore. She had some cash saved up from her last job, but she had not recovered from the trauma of how that job—and the relationship it had entailed—had ended.

She made a cup of tea and sat down with her laptop. She pulled up Google and ran a search for Mitchell Beck. There was plenty of information about him: he was a self-made millionaire who would likely be a billionaire if a few ventures hadn't folded up on him five years ago. She only found a few articles that painted him as untrustworthy. He had been charged with conspiracy to bribe a state college in order to get his nephew into Harvard. He had also been caught with a prostitute on two occasions. But the one that seemed to line up with the case was the story that did its best to pin him to two different drug cartels—one in New York and one in Arizona. According to the article, he'd actually been charged for it at one point but the charges were dropped several days after he had been taken into custody. None of the articles she found detailing the events explained why he was let go.

After about half an hour of this, she shut the laptop down and started cleaning up the remaining mess from Danielle's break-in. As she did, her mind kept turning to the darker years her sister had suffered through. Back in those days, from the age of fourteen to just a few years ago, something like breaking into her sister's apartment might not have seemed like such a big deal to Danielle. But Chloe had seen real progress lately, especially after they had reunited to try to find the truth about their mother.

But something was clearly different now. While Danielle was indeed being the supportive sister Chloe had always wanted, she was definitely slipping back into her old ways. Chloe thought about what might have changed and then a possibility settled in over her mind. Actually, it was more than a possibility … it was almost a certainty. It made too much sense to simply ignore.

Has Danielle stopped taking her meds?

She recalled how Danielle was so annoyed that she had to take the medicine when the two of them had started reconciling. They'd always made her think something was wrong with her. Though, to be fair, there was: she'd been diagnosed with borderline personality disorder at the age of fifteen.

Suddenly very worried, Chloe tried calling Danielle again. For the second time, it went straight to voicemail. Her first instinct was to ride to Danielle's apartment, but she knew that would be a mistake. Whenever Danielle did not want to be bothered, she *really* did not want to be bothered. When she went into introvert mode, it was intentional. Chloe supposed it made sense; she was probably embarrassed about breaking into Chloe's apartment and was still processing all the emotion that came with it.

To occupy her mind, she kept cleaning the apartment. She was nearly done with it when the weight of worry became too much. She picked up her phone and simply stared at it for a moment. She called Danielle again but to the exact same results. She then found herself growing angry with Agent Moulton for not being available for her. She then considered Dr. Fischer but the idea of calling twice in consecutive days was just too sad. Grimacing, she scrolled to Rhodes's number and pressed CALL.

The phone rang three times and then went to voicemail. She thought about leaving a message but decided against it. Rhodes was probably actually *enjoying* her afternoon off after the last few days they'd spent. *Must be nice,* Chloe thought.

For the next hour or so, she kept looking at her phone, thinking of trying Danielle again. But each time she thought about it, the urge to just go to her apartment grew stronger, so she eventually stopped.

When her phone rang at 6:05, she practically raced across the living room to grab it from its place on the kitchen counter. Her heart broke a bit when she did not see Danielle's name on the display. It then surged with hope and excitement when she saw Johnson's name.

"This is Agent Fine," she answered.

"Fine, it's Johnson. Look…I wish I had better news and I wish I wasn't so pissed off to tell you what I'm about to tell you."

"What is it? What's wrong?"

"We have to let Alejos go."

"What?"

"There was some massive screw-up in New York. I'm still getting details as they come in but it looks like the evidence we thought we had against him is flimsy at best. It's falling like a house of cards."

"What about the phone records?" Chloe asked. "That should be enough to at least hold him for suspicion of murder."

"You're right. And right now, we're trying to angle things in a way where that would be the primary charge. If we can hold him a bit longer under that premise, we're hoping whatever was messed up in New York can be resolved. Keller and Labitski are working to that end right now."

"So what do you need me to do?"

"Nothing. Just sit tight. I may have you and Rhodes go back to Falls Church to investigate if we can get an exact triangulation on where the incoming call was received from. I've got Moxley and a team working on that right now. Would you call Rhodes and fill her in?"

"Okay," Chloe said and killed the call.

She looked around the apartment and let out a rather loud expletive. She tried Rhodes again and this time, her partner answered.

"You just can't stand to eb apart from me, huh?" Rhodes said.

"Johnson just called. The charges against Alejos are falling apart."

"What?"

She then recited everything Johnson had just told her, putting emphasis on the fact that he was still being held by a thread based on his possible involvement in the murder of Jessie Fairchild.

"Our system is fucked," Rhodes said.

"That's putting it mildly."

"Want to go grab a beer or ten?" Rhodes said.

"No. I'm just…."

"Chloe…I know there's something else, too. Whatever that thing is that you wouldn't go into detail about earlier. Level with me…are you okay?"

She hesitated before answering. She didn't see the point in lying anymore. The more she lied to others, the easier it was for her to believe the lies. "I don't know. I think I will be eventually. There's just some family stuff going on right now…stuff that sort of got mirrored in this Fairchild case."

"Want to talk about it?"

"I probably should, but I'm not ready just yet."

There was a silence on the other end before Rhodes finally said, "Okay. Just…I know it might be weird, but I'm here if you ever want to vent about it."

"I know. Thanks."

They ended the call, leaving Chloe in a quiet apartment again. She thought of Danielle, holed up alone with her phone turned off. She thought of Julio Alejos, probably smirking at everyone who went into his interrogation room. And she thought of her father, watching him through his back kitchen window, living a life of normalcy.

Lastly, she brought the image of Jessica Fairchild to mind, her throat butchered by the ring, bruised by the fox sole.

She picked up the teacup she had been using earlier and looked at it thoughtfully. She then heaved it hard across the room, where it exploded against the wall. It wasn't the most mature reaction but the sound of shattering was perhaps the most therapeutic thing for her in that moment.

She only allowed herself a few seconds of this feeling, though. She grabbed her broom and dustpan and instantly cleaned up the mess, realizing as she did that it seemed to be the perfect illustration for this stage of her life: always cleaning up a mess, always picking up the pieces.

No more than twenty minutes had passed after she had shattered the cup when someone knocked at her door. Her heart leaped, surging with certainty. The sister instinct within her *knew* that this was Danielle. Danielle had her phone off and had turned it on to see that her sister had called three times, clearly worried about her.

Chloe sprinted to the door and then calmed herself a bit before answering. She didn't want Danielle seeing just how anxious she was, how worried she had been for the last few hours. She took a deep breath, collected herself, and opened the door.

Before she even had a chance to peer out into the hallway, the door came slamming back against her. Her left arm got caught between her body, crushing it against her. The action was so unexpected that Chloe wasn't even able to comprehend what had happened until she fell to the floor on her back. Her mind raced to keep up and came to only the simplest of conclusions.

Not Danielle.

Someone's attacking me…

The second thought was what brought her fully to her senses. By then, though, whoever had slammed the door into her was falling down on top of her. She caught an elbow to the chest and the wind went rushing out of her. She then felt the full weight of her attacker on top of her. They both wrestled for position but the surprise of the attack and being pinned beneath his body put Chloe at a severe disadvantage.

As she tried her best to gain the advantage, he drove a knee hard into her hip. As she tried to slide away from that attack, she then felt an elbow slam into her side. Again, more wind went rushing out of her. As she gasped, she felt the weight of her attacker come off of her but the relief was minor and barely registered at all as she then felt a pair of vise-like hands wrap around her throat.

She was very much aware that the attacker knew what they were doing. The surprise element at the start, expertly pinning her down by lying on top of her, knocking the wind out of her before going for the throat. He had done this before—perhaps several times.

She could tell by the build and sheer strength that her attacker was male. His face was like stone, staring coldly at her as he strangled her. His blond hair was pulled back into a small ponytail which barely moved at all as he perched rigidly on top of her.

Chloe felt her body tensing up. She drew her arms up, trying to punch at the man. She tried throwing a hard palm strike directly upward into his chin but he was arched back just enough for the strike to miss—further proof that he was no stranger to what he was doing. She kicked her feet out, hoping to find something to rest her foot on to push herself… anything to move, to make the attacker have to move the slightest bit to maintain his position.

But there was nothing. Her feet kicked out at empty space, her right toe just barely striking one of her barstools. She tried pushing her elbows against the floor to force herself into a half-sitting position but when she did so, the attacker pressed down harder, making the movement hurt her elbows as she tried to push.

She felt something being pinched in her throat. Excruciating pain swept through it as she tried to draw in a breath. She saw little white dots in her vision as her lungs begged for air. She winced, fearing that the man might actually break her neck before he managed to strangle her.

She felt the fight rushing out of her. The pain in her neck was second only to the pain in her lungs, now desperate for air.

Then, somehow, miraculously, his grip around her neck was gone. At the same time, she was doused in something wet, in something that smelled bitter. She had no time to figure out what had happened, though; as soon as she realized she was free, she used her elbows to push away from him. It was easier than she had anticipated because he was slowly falling over away from her.

What the hell?

But then she saw what had happened. It might have been funny any other time but in that moment, it was all business.

Rhodes stood over the attacker. She held the neck of a wine bottle in her hand, dripping red wine. The rest of the bottle was littered over the floor and the attacker. Most of the wine had splattered to the floor, but a great deal of it was on the back of his head.

Common sense told her what had happened: Rhodes came over with a bottle of wine, probably trying to be a good friend during a time of weird emotions. Seeing what was going down on the kitchen floor, she had blasted the attacker over the back of the head with the bottle of wine.

But even as Chloe registered all of this, things changed drastically. Rhodes leaned down to place a restraint hold on the man but he was ready for it. When she tried latching her arm around his neck, he grabbed her arm, wrenched it, and curled himself into a hard ducking motion. The result was Rhodes flipping over his shoulder, directly in the wine and broken glass.

Chloe sat up and tried getting to her feet, but her body was not having it. Her lungs were still aching and her brain was still convinced that death was only a few moments away. The world swam in front of her eyes and she nearly pitched forward on her face when she tried to stand.

Meanwhile, the attacker was now dropping down on Rhodes. Only before he could land, Rhodes got a knee up. It threw him to the side just enough for Rhodes to roll away. But the man was incredibly fast. He came charging at her, nearly leaping.

Rhodes stopped him with a rapid kick to the face, a kick that came so quickly it was like watching a rabbit. The kick stunned the man for just a moment. As he shook it off and came at her again, Rhodes repeated the motion, this time throwing out two kicks with rapid speed. The first created a crunching noise that broke the man's nose. The second sent a jettison of blood down the man's face.

He roared and instantly retreated. Rhodes got up to give chase but the man threw an elbow behind him which caught her in the side of the head. Rhodes went stumbling backward, catching herself on the back of the couch. Chloe could see where some of the glass from the shattered wine bottle was bitten into her arm.

Chloe then watched as the attacker retreated through the door, taking a left to head back down the hallway. Chloe stumbled up to her knees, trying to use the couch as support.

"Chloe, where's your gun?" Rhodes said. "I don't have mine."

"Bedroom. Dresser…"

She managed to finally rise up to her feet, wobbling against the couch. By the time she regained some semblance of strength and balance, Rhodes had retrieved the Glock from its place in her bedroom and started rushing for the front door. Chloe wanted to call out to her but the two words she had just spoken felt like it had torn her sore throat into shreds.

She could only watch, slowly regaining her breath and her strength as Rhodes raced out the door, headed in the same direction as the man who had nearly killed Chloe less than a minute ago.

CHAPTER THIRTY

Several second after Rhodes left in pursuit of the blond man with the ponytail, Chloe scrambled over to the kitchen counter. She grabbed her phone and called Assistant Director Garcia, knowing full well she stood a better chance of getting him on the phone than she did Johnson. Garcia did answer, and right away. Chloe did her best to get the words out, her throat still aching terribly.

"I was attacked. Rhodes is in pursuit on foot. My apartment building…"

She simply could not get any more words out. She ended the call, confident that Garcia would send someone over to assist.

In the meantime, Chloe could not just allow Rhodes to risk her life for her. She knew it was a bad idea, but she went racing out the door and broke off in the same direction Rhodes and her assailant had headed. With each step, her legs seemed to get a bit braver and her brain started to realize that it was indeed alive and there was a job to get done.

She could hear footfalls ahead of her, from the stairway. The sound of it sent a jolt of adrenaline through her and her legs were much more trustworthy as she came to the stairs. She hurried down them as quickly as she could. As she made it halfway down, she heard Rhodes yell out from what sounded like the lobby: "FBI, move to the side!"

Chloe instinctually reached for her sidearm, realizing stupidly that it wasn't there; she had told Rhodes to take it.

She came to the bottom of the stairs, her lungs aching as a reminder of what they had endured less than three minutes ago.

She allowed herself just a moment to rest. She saw a woman and her child, no older than ten, down on the lobby floor and pressed against the wall—presumably the people Rhodes had yelled at second ago. Chloe then looked ahead, through the building's glass doors. Outside, night had just started to fall, but she could clearly see Rhodes crossing the street, the gun still drawn.

Chloe went out after her but by the time she reached the sidewalk, Rhodes was out of view. Chloe ran in the direction she had last seen her, ignoring the traffic and the few pedestrians who looked around wildly, having noticed that something dangerous was afoot. It was because of these people that Chloe was able to understand where Rhodes and her assailant had gone. Halfway down the block across from her street, a small alley cut between a Chinese restaurant and a small overpriced antiques store. Chloe ran for the alleyway, her legs now working to their maximum, but her lungs still struggling.

As she rounded the corner and entered the alley she saw that the attacker had somehow gotten the drop on Rhodes. They were fighting against the side of the antiques store, Rhodes pinned to it while the attacker drove a hard right fist into her stomach. Chloe watched as Rhodes buckled. When she did, the attacker grabbed her right wrist and twisted it hard, trying to get her to drop the gun.

Sure enough, she did. The moment it clattered to the ground, the man punched Rhodes in the face. She stumbled a bit to the right, managing to keep herself upright against the wall. As the man reached for the gun, his back slightly turned to Chloe, Chloe took off at a full sprint. She felt like she was having to work for each breath she drew in but she barreled on anyway.

The attacker sensed her coming when she was about ten feet away. He had not yet come up with the Glock; he was still slightly bent over and peering back at her. He hurried a bit but being distracted by Chloe made him momentarily lose the grip on the Glock.

That was the window of opportunity she needed. She dove for him, faking a high strike but switching at the last moment. Her shoulders collided with his legs, just below the knees. He went down in a heap, right on top of her. He fought for purchase, trying to strike her in the back, but it was poorly aimed, thrown in haste, and barely grazed her side.

In the tangle of arms and legs, Chloe spotted her Glock, lying about five feet away. She scrambled for it, her hand gripping it just as the man brought a hard knee down on her back.

Chloe screamed out in pain, waiting for another blow, but it never came. Instead, Rhodes locked the man in a headlock from behind, wrapping her arm around his neck and trying to drag him to the ground. Like Chloe before her, though, Rhodes was not prepared for the man's brute strength. With one hard lunge, he backed into the wall of the Chinese restaurant, smashing Rhodes. Chloe could hear the back of her partner's head slam into the brick. She lost her grip on the man's neck and he wheeled around to catch her. He grabbed her by the hair and drew her head back as she tried to get back to her feet.

He's going to smash her skull against the brick, Chloe thought.

It was a thought that made her next option a clear one. There might be repercussions later, but so be it.

Before the man could shove Rhodes's head forward, Chloe drew up the Glock, took aim, and fired. The shot took him in the side of the head, rocking his body from the chest up hard to the right. From such close range, Chloe also saw the results of the bullet's exit but looked away quickly.

She kept the gun pointed at his fallen body, but it was clear that he was not getting up. She looked over at Rhodes. Some of the man's blood was splattered across her forehead and her eyes were wide with shock. She got to her feet slowly, leaning against the wall and looking at the fallen man.

"Who is it?" Rhodes asked.

"Don't know," Chloe said. The words seemed even harder to squeeze out now. But in her head, she guessed it was someone who worked for Alejos. Perhaps even the man who had killed Jessie Fairchild.

She looked at his blond ponytail, now stained with blood, and it started to slowly click into place.

But when she heard sirens in the distance—likely the cavalry sent by Garcia—she stopped trying to piece it altogether. She lay on the ground, her eyes locked on Rhodes, and listened to the sirens draw closer.

CHAPTER THIRTY ONE

Roughly three hours after Chloe had put a bullet into the head of the man who had attacked her in her apartment, Julio Alejos put in a request to speak with Chloe. Though she was up for it and wanted answers, Johnson ordered her to reject it. Besides, it was hard to accept such a request when she was being treated and tended to in the hospital.

As it turned out, she had been incredibly lucky. She had a massive bruise on her back and multiple bruises still forming and changing colors on her neck. There had been several X-rays and tests done, but nothing had been broken. Her windpipe showed signs of stress but it had not been majorly damaged. The doctors had asked her to lay off on overblown talking for the next few days, and she was fine with that.

She was awaiting results on the final test for her throat when there was a knock at the door. She looked to the doorway and was surprised to see Director Johnson standing there.

"I hear you might be out of here pretty soon," he said.

She nodded. She pointed to her throat, then to her mouth, and shook her head.

"Yeah, I know you're not supposed to talk. The doctors already told me."

She nodded and then managed to get out a single word: "Rhodes?"

"I think she got it worse than you. A nasty bump on her head, a mild concussion, and seven stitches for a cut on her arm. She says she brought the wine to your place because she was trying to cheer you up. Everything okay?"

Chloe only shrugged.

"Well, I come bringing some decent news. Once we told Alejos that you had been attacked and that the attacker ended up getting killed, he was a little more open to talking. I think that's why he asked for you. He was a little more forthcoming. The forensics results helped, too."

Chloe tilted her head and raised her eyebrows. "Forensics?"

"They took a hair sample from the attacker ... whose name was Deacon Galimore, by the way. He had a long history of drug trafficking in New York and was a known friend of Alejos. Mitchell Beck, too, it seems. Anyway, Alejos says Mark Fairchild got greedy ... tried to blackmail some of Alejos's men and embezzle some of their money. Apparently, he was successful. Alejos says it was a matter of about five hundred grand or so. And apparently, five hundred grand buys a dead wife. Julio admitted to sending Galimore to kill Jessie Fairchild ... a way to get back at Mark. Retribution or whatever. Anyway ... the hair samples from Galimore match the ones you found at the crime scene."

"So what happens to—" she started.

"Stop talking," Johnson interrupted. "He has asked for a few more hours to stew in it. He's trying to make a deal ... information on his cartel in exchange for enough information to not only find Mitchell Beck, but to put him away for good. He says Beck is behind a string of unsolved murders from ten years back and that he's also got his hands in a human trafficking ring. Alejos says there are a lot of public figures—politicians and entertainers—linked to Beck. It could be very big ... which is why Alejos might get whatever deal he asks for."

Chloe rolled her eyes.

"I agree. Anyway ... whatever he decides, whatever deal is struck, the Jessie Fairchild case is closed. Right now, we're just trying to nail down the convictions for Mark Fairchild and Alejos. You did some great work, Agent Fine. Rhodes said you basically saved her life. You know ... that'll be the second time, right?"

"Who's counting?"

"I'm pretty sure Rhodes is."

With that, Johnson gave her a smile and headed back out. Chloe watched him go, trying to find some happiness in the update he had just given her. Jessie's killer had been found and taken care of. Mark would be facing some time for his involvement, and she and Rhodes had not only helped to start the dissolution of a huge drug cartel, but also played a hand in what could lead to the exposure of a highly sought after professional criminal in Mitchell Beck.

Yes, it all sounded good and she figured at some point, she'd soak it all up and manage to be proud.

But her mind was already turning back to Danielle. She still wasn't answering her phone, and with every hour that passed, Chloe became more and more worried about her.

She also could not help but think of her father. Somewhere ahead, there was a very rough moment for the three of them. Maybe once that was over and done with, Chloe would be able to resume her normal life, could work on violent cases without her judgment being clouded by her own drama.

But until that day came, she had to own it and not let it ruin her in the process.

EPILOGUE

At 1:15 in the morning, while her sister was being discharged from a Washington, DC, hospital, Danielle Fine crossed the Oklahoma/Texas state line. She was tired and hungry, but she knew she could not stop.

Her father had been making noises in the trunk for the last hour or so. She had turned up her music, some loud and abrasive stuff from her teenage years, to drown it out. It had worked, and she had allowed herself to drive in a sort of hypnotic state as the night lured her on.

She knew she'd have to stop for gas soon. And that was fine...she'd pull off onto some little two-lane stretch of nothing and fill up at a convenience store in a no-name town. There would be less traffic and far less chance of anyone hearing the whining and complaining of the man in her trunk. She'd stopped in Tennessee and taped his mouth shut. She'd also reinforced the duct tape along the edges of the quilt. She'd thought about giving him water, but in the end decided fuck it. He could go without.

And now he was moaning again, through the tape. She could hear it even through the brazen bass drum of the industrial music that flooded the car.

She turned down the music and waited a moment.

"Dad, can you hear me?"

There was no response from the trunk. She slammed on the brakes, stopping in the middle of the two-lane. There was no traffic coming from either direction, allowing her to be a bit reckless. Of course, she stayed her course in terms of the speed limit. It would be terrible to be pulled over by the police, given what she was carrying in the trunk.

The jostling noise in the back from slamming on the brakes made her smile. "I said, can you hear me?"

This time, she got a slight response.

"I'm going to let you out soon enough," she said. "We're almost there. And when we get there, you and I are going to sit and have a nice heart to heart. Sound good?"

She got no answer but that was okay. She knew he could hear her.

"Hold on," she said with a smile.

She hit the gas and started forward again. If her father continued his complaints, she did not hear. She turned the music back up and was reminded of her younger years as a teenager, when she didn't have a care in the world. She supposed that even back then she had been planning this moment. She smiled at the synchronicity of it all as she drove through the night, forest on both sides and stars above.

The night road looked long and endless ahead of her and that was fine with her. With her father bound up in the trunk and her future once again in her own hands, Danielle was feeling better than she had in a very long time.

Now Available for Pre-Order!

HOMECOMING
(A Chloe Fine Psychological Suspense Mystery—Book 5)

"A masterpiece of thriller and mystery. Blake Pierce did a magnificent job developing characters with a psychological side so well described that we feel inside their minds, follow their fears and cheer for their success. Full of twists, this book will keep you awake until the turn of the last page."
—Books and Movie Reviews, Roberto Mattos (re Once Gone)

HOMECOMING (A Chloe Fine Mystery) is book #5 in a new psychological suspense series by bestselling author Blake Pierce, whose #1 bestseller Once Gone (Book #1) (a free download) has over 1,000 five-star reviews.

When two husbands, best friends, turn up dead in a wealthy suburban town, FBI VICAP Special Agent Chloe Fine, 27, is called in to unmask the lies in this small town and to find the killer.

Chloe will have to penetrate this town's perfect façade, to get past its public appearances to understand the truth of who these men were, and who may have wanted them dead. And in a town that thrives on its exclusivity, that won't be easy to do.

What secrets were these husbands hiding?

An emotionally wrought psychological suspense with layered characters, small-town ambiance and heart-pounding suspense, HOMECOMING is book #5 in a riveting new series that will leave you turning pages late into the night.

Book #6 in the Chloe Fine series will also be available soon.

HOMECOMING
(A Chloe Fine Psychological Suspense Mystery—Book 5)

Did you know that I've written multiple novels in the mystery genre? If you haven't read all my series, click the image below to download a series starter!